For Jodi,

With best wishes

Bashir

MAARGIR

The Snake Charmer

BASHIR SAKHAWARZ

PLATINUM PRESS

ISBN 978-93-81576-25-0

Cover Design Fravashi Aga
Layouts Ajay Shah
Printing Repro India Ltd

Published in India 2013 by
PLATINUM PRESS
An imprint of
LEADSTART PUBLISHING PVT LTD
Trade Centre, Level 1, Bandra Kurla Complex
Bandra (E), Mumbai 400 051, INDIA
T + 91 22 40700804 **F** +91 22 40700800
E info@leadstartcorp.com **W** www.leadstartcorp.com

US Office
Axis Corp, 7845 E Oakbrook Circle, Madison, WI 53717, USA

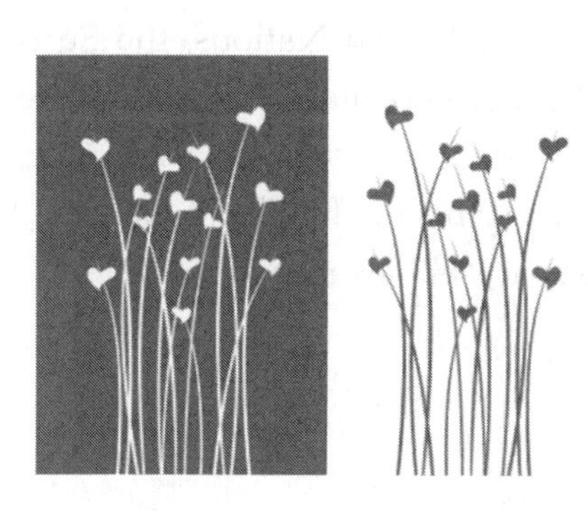

To my mother Bibi Gul
and my wife Romana Rauf
~ for their unconditional love.

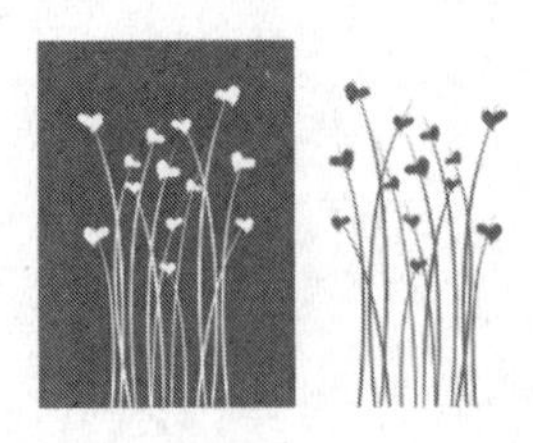

ABOUT THE AUTHOR

Bashir Sakhawarz is an award-winning poet, novelist and short story writer. A native of worntorn Afghanistan, he has lived in Europe, Asia, Africa and Central America and worked for international organizations such as the United Nations, the European Union, the Asian Development Bank, The International Red Cross and NGOS.

Bashir Sakhawarz lives with his family in Geneva, Switzerland. He can be reached at: bashir_sakhawarz@yahoo.ie

CHAPTER 1

The choice was either the snake charmer or the doctor. Hamid decided to choose the doctor. To ignore the snake charmer and take his brother to a qualified doctor was unconventional. But he was making the choice to save his brother.

It was some time since his brother had lost his appetite and the colour of his eyes had changed to yellow, a clear sign that Rahmat was suffering from hepatitis. Hamid was asked by his parents to take Rahmat to the snake charmer who had a shop at the end of their street. The snake charmer was not only famous for catching the most dangerous snakes such as the red skinned cobra, but was also a well known healer who could help his patients with all sorts of problems. He had saved the lives of people bitten by snakes and assisted women yearning to get pregnant. Legend had it that he could cure thousands of diseases including hepatitis.

Hamid's parents were deeply religious. They believed in rituals and the snake charmer- cum-healer was their first choice for treating illnesses. With God's help and the power of belief many sick people were cured after a visit to the snake charmer. A huge man, with dark skin, big lips and a long beard, and a most impressive appearance, he attracted people from all walks of life. His shop was bursting with boxes in which he kept dangerous snakes. From time to time he opened one of these and charmed a snake into showing its face to patients. Sometimes, he encouraged the snakes to ready themselves for attack, but controlled them when anyone was startled. He loved these games and could see that his patients were mesmerised, convinced of the amazing power of his dark eyes – the power of controlling dangerous snakes. Yet, faced with his brother's malady, Hamid opted to go to a conventional doctor whom he had met at a wedding two months ago.

"Are you sure it's the right choice?" Rahmat asked.

Hamid looked squarely at him. "I think the doctor will cure you."

Rahmat wiped his hand across his forehead, hot with a thin film of sweat. "It's only that I… I feel afraid that…" His voice trailed off.

"You'll feel better when you get well." Hamid clasped his brother's shoulder. "I won't let you down."

Hamid sounded confident but perhaps he was not so sure. Prior to the wedding Hamid had passed Doctor Nasrat occasionally along the narrow alleys where they lived. As was the custom of the good people of Andrabi, they greeted each other politely. It was at the wedding party that someone had spoken about the ability of the local snake charmer to cure the most untreatable sicknesses. Other people in the room agreed that, indeed, God had given him the gift of healing and the power to bring almost dead people back to life. Doctor Nasrat, a graduate of the university hospital in Moscow, listened to these enthusiastic stories without participating in the conversation. Finally, he could no longer restrain himself from saying that the snake charmer was nothing but a con artist. He tried hard to convince them that in today's world there was no place for superstition. This response shocked the wedding guests. They believed in the snake charmer's powers and were unhappy with allegations of quackery. For the past 25 years it was he who had treated and cured the inhabitants of Andrabi, not the medical doctor. Nobody believed a doctor was superior to a snake charmer. In fact, they concluded in their hearts that the doctor was probably jealous of his popularity, whose waiting room was packed with visitors from all over the country, whereas no one even knew where Doctor Nasrat's clinic was located.

Hamid listened attentively to the medical doctor, as he had faith in education. In his school, teaching was scientific and there was no place for people like snake charmers. His science teacher talked about the latest developments of the world, modern technology and even medicine, which was new in a country where most of the people listened to preachers and believed in healers and snake charmers; in a country where mullahs did not believe that Neil Armstrong had landed on moon saying 'the moon is a holy place and no infidel can step on it'. Hamid felt a bond with Doctor Nasrat. They talked at length at the wedding party and both realized that they got on well together. The doctor invited him to come to his clinic for a cup of tea and to talk about his philosophy of life. Hamid had gracefully accepted, but put off visiting him.

It was late afternoon as Hamid and Rahmat reached Doctor Nasrat's clinic and found the doctor alone, sitting in an armchair. He looked up from reading the newspaper. "What a surprise!"

Hamid felt embarrassed not to have visited him before. "I was planning to come earlier, but have been so busy at school. I'm preparing for my exams for university entrance, and I haven't had the time." It was the best excuse he could think of.

"What subjects are you studying?"

"Literature. I spend most of my time in the public library reading books. I want to study literature and become a writer."

"That's good, the country certainly needs good writers, who can understand the people and guide them with wise words."

"I'm not sure if I'll ever become a good writer, but I love reading and writing."

"If you study hard and read the right material you will certainly become a good writer one day."

The doctor turned to look at Rahmat's pale face. "But I don't think you came here today to tell me about your future career."

Hamid was relieved that finally the doctor would allow him to explain their visit.

"My brother Rahmat is sick. He hasn't eaten much these last few days and he feels very tired."

Doctor Nasrat was in his early thirties but even at that young age most of his hair was already grey. Tall and slim, he did not follow the fashion of the time and dressed modestly. He was wearing a grey suite which somehow matched his grey hair and made him look handsome.

"Sit down here," he indicated a chair to Rahmat, and started to examine him. He looked closely at his eyes, his throat, his ears; he put his stethoscope on his chest and then suggested that a blood sample should be tested in a laboratory.

"Yes. You have hepatitis, but maybe there might be other complications."

Hamid was troubled. He realized the reason why most people preferred the snake charmer. It did not cost as much, the homemade medicines were cheaper and he never asked patients for tests. As if the doctor could read the worry in Hamid's face, he explained, "The man in charge of the laboratory is one of our comrades. He will not take money from you and you don't need to bother about the cost of the medicines. I will help you with that. I will give you some drugs which should cure it. There is no charge."

"But Doctor Nasrat I cannot accept your kind gesture. I should be able to pay." Hamid responded with embarrassment.

"Would you take money from a poor man for reading one of your articles? Dear Comrade, we are not here to make a profit. We are here to help people in need."

The doctor counted out tablets into a small bottle and handed them to Rahmat. "These are new drugs from Russia, they should work well."

As the two brothers began to leave, the doctor handed a book to Hamid. It was a novel called 'Mother' written by Maxim Gorky.

"Read it and tell me what you think of it by next Friday evening. We will meet in one of the comrades' house. I will drop by to pick you up."

Half-way home, Rahmat stopped in the street to face Hamid. "Thank you," he said quietly. "I won't say anything at home."

Hamid was not so preoccupied with what to tell their parents, but was reflecting more on what the doctor had mentioned. His mind was busy thinking, 'Why had the doctor been so generous? Why had he used the word comrade to address him? What did this reference to comrade imply?' Above all he was intrigued about the purpose of Friday's meeting.

The night passed without further incident. Rahmat who was only two years younger than Hamid, respected his elder brother and never disobeyed him. He also had faith in his brother. That was the reason why when Hamid told him that the snake charmer was not the right person to cure his illness, Rahmat agreed. Taking Rahmat to the medical doctor was not only because Hamid did not believe in superstition, but there also was another reason. He loved his brother and wanted to make sure that he was cured properly. For him modern medicine was the only way to help Rahmat. During the visit to the doctor, Rahmat kept quiet and only spoke when the doctor asked him about his health. He had a quiet nature and always kept his opinion to himself, not like Hamid who was outspoken. He also went to modern school and yet he felt science was a tool, which could explain Islam well. He was religious, but like his brother knew that the snake charmer had nothing to do with religion and curing people.

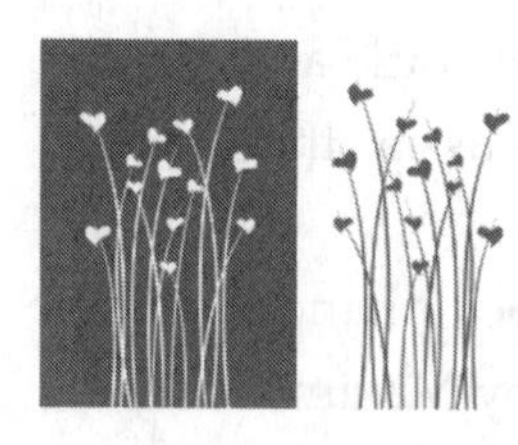

CHAPTER 2

"Thank you Allah for making me healthy again," said Rahmat, and kissed the white marble stone with Koranic inscriptions.

Here lies the king of Islam who sacrificed his life for Allah, his spirit is surrounded with rays coming from heaven.

Halima, their mother, was happy that her sons had been to the snake charmer and that he had cured Rahmat from the horrible illness. But now she had given them a new task; to thank Allah by going to the nearest shrine, *Shah-e do Shamshaira,* to take some *halwa* that she had cooked to give to the poor who gather at the shrine.

"Rahmat, we know nothing about these shrines." Hamid was standing behind Rahmat. "What do you mean?"

"I was in the library the other day and happened to pick up a book about the local history of shrines in Andrabi."

"So what did you find?"

"Well, the *Peer-e Boland* shrine has nothing to do with Islam?"

"You mean the place mother took us to every Wednesday to thank Allah?"

"Yes! You know nobody is buried there."

"What! It's not possible."

"Yes, I'm serious. When the British were leaving Kabul after their defeat in 1842, they realized that they couldn't take their heavy weapons with them. So they buried them on the top of the hill, fixed a flag on it and named it the shrine of *Peer-e-Boland;* the holy man on the top the hill, to keep it safe."

"I don't believe you!"

"If you don't believe me, don't. The place was intact until they invaded Kabul again. They opened up the hole and took all the weapons out, but kept it as a shrine to make sure no one suspected anything."

"And now poor women are swallowing the dust of the shrine?"

"Yes. They're stupid! They're swallowing the dust created by the British."

"So you're telling me that *Shah-e do Shamshaira* is also a fake person?"

"No, thanks to Allah it's not fake; otherwise you and I would have finished the *halwa* together, because I wouldn't let mother's *halwa* go to waste."

"So what's the story behind this shrine?"

"He was Arab."

"What! I thought he was Afghan."

"What Afghan! We were all Hindus in those days. When the Arabs came to convert our people to Islam, they fought hard. And all their soldiers and their commander, *Shah-e do Shamshaira,* the leader with two swords, were massacred. They were buried where they fell and later when houses were built on the graveyard, the people kept the shrines."

"Don't tell me we were Hindus?"

"Yes, we were Hindus and today on *shab-e baraat* we remember the death of the Muslims who were martyred. The book I was reading explains that *shabe-e baraat,* the sacred night, is the night of deliverance and we observe it with a nightlong vigil of prayers. That's why we light candles every Friday night. Andrabi's famous for being a town of shrines and the graveyard of martyrs."

They walked back home along the narrow streets avoiding the wider streets used by cars. They arrived at the central square. Children were playing *topdanda,* similar to baseball, and some others were running around playing catch. The square was located at walking distance of less than 5 to 10 minutes from any house and was used for many activities. It was also a car park in all seasons. Sometimes, adults played football or volleyball. During Eid children brought boiled eggs and challenged each other to an egg fight. One child would hit the tip of the egg of the other child, being careful of the impact on his own egg. The first eggshell that cracked was the loser. The winner took the egg of the loser. In winter, the square became a ground for other sports. Boys indulged in snowball fights or joined in ice-skating.

As they passed the mosque, a beautiful musical recital captured their ears. The sound of the Koran recitation occurred after early morning prayers at dawn when the children came to the mosque to learn to recite the Koran and in the evening. The mullah taught them with a melodious voice and they repeated the verses. Andrabi was very spiritual.

As they passed the north gate, Hamid turned to his brother, and said, "I discovered other things from the book that I was reading."

"Please don't knock my faith."

"No, this gate reminds me of the history of Andrabi. Andrabi was part of the old city where guerillas fought against the British for Afghanistan's independence some 130 years ago. It had two main gates: this one in the north, on the edge of the river and the other in the south, facing the mountains. Here was the best place for the Afghans to attack the British, and then they disappeared in the mountains to the south. Now the gates have gone."

"It's a shame."

"Well they don't serve their purpose any longer. They used to keep Kabul safe. Now it is the responsibility of the government and the police force to provide security and gates are no longer necessary. The city entrance and exit is left open through the night for people to get in and out."

Andrabi was changing even if no one could see it. Houses were built of mud, stone and wood and lasted for a long time. So what had changed in Andrabi if it was not the landscape? It was the people. Gone were the days when the centre of education had been the mosque. Today, parents sent their children to school and some even went on to university. Such cultural changes met with resistance by the traditionalists and religious people, led by the mullahs of the mosques, who were not happy with this change of direction. After the codetta and the change of government from a monarchy to a republic in 1973, changes in the attitudes of the people became even more apparent. They really felt that the best future for their children was a proper education and that the new government should assist the new generation's formal schooling. So it was the soul of Andrabi, the people that were changing. Some clung with traditional values, some claimed modernisation.

The other change was the influx of migrants to Andrabi. People, mainly from the northern villages of Afghanistan, migrated to the old part of Kabul and found Andrabi to be a favourite destination. Andrabi was in the heart of Kabul. The arrival of the new population created a class structure that had not existed before. The indigenous occupants of Andrabi referred to themselves as the real Kabulis, which in fact they were, and they called the new arrivals immigrants. In making decisions related to the community of Andrabi, the Kabulis had the upper hand.

Hamid and his family belonged to the upper class and were real Kabulis. His father, Abdul, had a small grocery shop near the mosque and spent his time between the house, his shop and the mosque. His two sons were taken to the mosque at a tender age, much earlier than school, to learn about Islamic teaching. Their father encouraged them, nurturing hopes for them to become government officers in the future with a strict religious upbringing. Hamid completed his primary education in the mosque under the apprenticeship of a famous mullah, a graduate of Deoband, India, before pursuing his formal school education. The second son, Rahmat, however, continued his Islamic studies parallel with his formal schooling. Hamid's parents were happy with both children and did not interfere with their choices. Continuing Islamic learning made their younger son Rahmat a fervently religious young man. Hamid, on the other hand, became more of a romantic, spending hours in the public library, writing poetry.

The Kabul public library was not far from Andrabi and Hamid could easily walk there whenever he wished. The reading rooms were crowded with whispering researchers and political activists. Hamid was thirsty for knowledge and frequently eavesdropped on the researchers to discover more literary work. Usually, he showed little interest in politics. However, one day he overheard the conversation of two young men addressing each other as comrade. It was unusual for people not to address each other by name, and Hamid's curiosity was piqued.

What would he discover at the meeting?

CHAPTER 3

Hamid was surprised to see Doctor Nasrat at his doorstep, suggesting that they go together to the Friday meeting. Hamid was looking forward to seeing the doctor again, but had not expected him to show up on the day the sky of the heavens had decided to open and pour out its heart. He had read the novel that the doctor had given him and was impressed by the Russian society it described. Before reading the book, Hamid had mainly focused on romantic poetry of classical Persian poets. He particularly enjoyed reading the poems called Epic of the Kings written by the great Persian poet Firdausi. It wasn't only the desire to discuss Gorky's novel that Hamid looked forward to. Curiosity was the other reason. He wanted to know more about the Friday meetings and the people that were involved; those who addressed each other as comrade.

They started walking in the rain using their umbrellas as protection. Few dared to venture out when it rained because it became very slippery. One had to focus on walking on the dirt roads and never losing concentration to avoid your clothes being covered with mud and water from an ungraceful fall. Idle spectators would frequently wait to observe the inevitable fall, always a matter of when rather than if, and they found much humour at the cost of the unfortunate victim. Of course it was impossible not to laugh. The people of Andrabi shared a common sense of humour and loved this game. Even if one survived falling on slippery paths, one would surely not escape the deluge from above. Many roof gutters channeled and discharged rainwater onto the middle of the small streets. For these reasons most people seldom left their houses when it rained. If they happened to be outside Andrabi, on the asphalt roads beyond the northern and southern entrances, they simply waited until the rain stopped. Sometimes it could take hours.

It was Friday – a Muslim public holiday in Afghanistan. God had his own schedule for sending heavy rain and this time He had chosen Friday. Men would only walk the short distance to their local mosque for prayers; otherwise they would stay at home.

Fortunately, the doctor was prepared. He had two umbrellas – one for himself and one for Hamid. They were soon making their passage through the narrow streets of Andrabi, overflowing with streams of rainwater. They successfully tackled the route without any falls and without being attacked by the water flowing from above. Then they boarded a bus towards the eastern part of Kabul.

When they reached their destination, the doctor looked quickly over his shoulder to observe if anyone had followed or watched them. They stood in front of a big wooden gate, painted light blue. Once Nasrat was reassured, he pressed the bell five times; three consecutive rings, a short gap and again two rings. Hamid realized that it was a coded message. Shortly afterwards a man opened the gate and greeted the doctor and Hamid. It was a big house with a wide open courtyard. They crossed the courtyard, went through a veranda and entered a large adjacent room. The room was bursting with men and women between the ages of twenty and forty. Hamid was nineteen and felt that he was the youngest. As was the custom of the country, the guests stood up and greeted each visitor warmly. The room was dense with smoke. He noticed that the walls were decorated with the photos of a bald man with a goatee beard and another man with a moustache that resembled Maxim Gorky. He also noticed a red flag hanging on the wall, which he recognized as the national flag of the Soviet Union.

Hamid was surprised to see women and men mingling together. Mixed gatherings only happened at weddings or at Eid celebrations and among the family members and friends only. But this was just an ordinary Friday. They sat cross-legged on the *toshak* with their backs supported by a pillow pressed against the wall. Most men were wearing caps and sported a moustache. Women were wearing western clothes such as skirts and blouses or jeans, but none of them were wearing makeup, which was unusual. Hamid wondered how the meeting would begin or what it would be about. Tea was served and everyone engaged in small talk. Suddenly the doctor raised his voice and addressed the gathering.

"Comrades, I am glad to introduce a new recruit, Comrade Hamid, who is an excellent writer and will be attending university next year. Some days ago I gave him the novel 'Mother' by Gorky and I would like you to listen to his views on this book. His feedback is significant given that it originates from a writer."

Hamid had not expected to be called upon to speak and suddenly felt shy. This was a new experience for him. He was not naturally reticent, but he felt embarrassed as he eyed the intelligent and sophisticated looking audience in the room. He swallowed hard and tried to overcome his nervousness.

"I am not really prepared and wasn't expecting to say anything. Not sure what I should say? I hope you don't mind and apologise if I didn't understand this book well. You see before reading Gorky I've been mainly enjoying poetry. I've just finished the romantic story of *Khosraw* and *Shireen*, by the poet Nezami, only a week ago. But this novel, the 'Mother', is totally different. It's a story about Russian society and how a working Russian woman turns into a revolutionary leader through oppression. It talks about her drunken husband and father. The mother and son fall victim to the Czar's troops. The inner meaning is about the growing struggle between capitalism and labour, which is far more widespread than just Russia. It could be synonymous for a story about a mother from Afghanistan."

Hamid continued speaking and then stopped. There was a long silence. He thought that he must have made a fool of himself and was about to apologise. Before he could do so, the doctor began clapping and the others followed.

"Welcome to our party Comrade Hamid. We need young men like you, with the understanding that you have just demonstrated. Today's meeting is for initiates and our gatherings are informal and without an agenda. We will help you understand the party and politics of our times, but before that let me introduce to you our leaders on the wall. The man with the beard is Vladimir Ilyich Lenin, the leader of the world's proletariat, and the other man with the moustache is Joseph Stalin. The flag, which I'm sure you recognize, is of the Soviet Union. In a way it represents all nations who are fighting for socialism and equality."

At that moment Hamid understood why the men were wearing caps and sported moustaches. They wanted to be Lenin look-alikes. During the meeting Hamid realized that he was watched by the male and female comrades as though being assessed. Hamid was neither tall, nor short. An ordinary looking man it seemed initially until he spoke. It was then that people would see him differently. The face appeared that of a young man, eyes gleaming with intelligence and knowledge, a face which gradually became more attractive as he spoke. His clothes were not expensive, but yet chosen with care; they exhibited elegant taste. He wore a camel tweed skinny blazer, which he had bought three years ago. A fountain pen on his top front pocket was placed quite eloquently. The discussion continued for hours. When they said goodbye to each other, Hamid was happy for three reasons. First, he had become a member of a progressive political party. Second, he now understood the meaning of the word comrade. Third, he had avoided the embarrassment of asking if the picture on the wall was Maxim Gorky.

CHAPTER 4

The two mulberry trees within the courtyard had been planted long before Nasrat or his mother were born. These trees were known to be moody since they followed the political situation of the country. Some years they bore fruit and others they stood erect, like massive fruitless trunks in the middle of the courtyard.

Hamid knocked on the main entrance door but no one answered. He continued knocking until finally Doctor Nasrat appeared on the rooftop, shouting, "Come up Hamid, I am flying pigeons."

"Doing what?"

"Come up, I will explain."

Hamid climbed up and saw that the Doctor's eyes were fixed on the sky, waving a net much bigger than the one used to catch fish.

Doctor Nasrat lived on a street not far from Hamid's home. His house was like the others, built with mud, but much smaller and less glamorous than Toftofi's. It only had two bedrooms. The street level was higher than the courtyard and when it rained, the water from the street flowed into his courtyard and not the other way around.

Flying pigeons was one of Nasrat's habits of relaxing, apart from reading books. He neither socialised with the people of Andrabi nor attended the mosque.

"You know Hamid jan, this habit probably originates from the Mughals. In India they also fly pigeons, but mostly among the Muslims. It is really relaxing to see birds fly in circles. My pigeons generally keep together and only rarely join the pigeons belonging to others."

Nasrat was waving the big net in similar motion to waving a flag, to ensure that the pigeons continued their flight. Hamid sometimes watched the pigeons and sometimes looked at Nasrat. His slim face, not shaved for a day or so made him look older than his age. Grey hair had appeared in his sideburns. His grey eyes matched the colour of his hair. He was wearing white *piran wa tonban.* Nasrat on the other hand was fully concentrating on flying the pigeons, focussing on the sights of the sky.

"Oh yes, I see that your pigeons mix with those of your neighbours."

"Yes, that is exactly when the sport starts. Sometimes my pigeons bring pigeons from those of other people and I have to catch the newcomers with my net before they can fly back. I keep the pigeon for a week or more until it gets used to the new place and then I fly that one too."

"Do you always win?"

"No, of course not. Yesterday I lost a beautiful *sabz patain.* I had paid a lot of money for it."

Hamid was fascinated by the scene of a serious man relaxing in this manner. He realised how fortunate that was, because half of the people in Andrabi spent their time smoking hashish or going to the cinema to watch Indian films and fall in love with the lead actresses. Doctor Nasrat knew how to relax without such drugs or association with people less intellectual. They had been on the roof for less than an hour, when Nasrat finally asked him to join him in the living room.

The living room walls were painted light green; from one hung a framed quotation from Lenin: *"Freedom in capitalist society always remains the same as it was in ancient Greek republics: Freedom for slave owners."* Shelves built into the walls were laden with books. The rosewood *almary,* standing next to the entrance door, had an air of the past, of glamorous inheritance, in contrast to the worn out sofas and the tea table with narrow legs. At the far corner a wood burner stove stood abandoned and unlit. The room smelled damp, as it lacked sunshine blocked by the large mulberry trees, though the big windows provided enough light that filtered in between the leaves. Nasrat played a record on the gramophone. It was a sad song.

"Do you know the meaning of this song?" Nasrat asked.

"Well, of course, I know. It is in Farsi!" Hamid laughed.

"Which is?"

"Come on Comrade, it simply says *'kiss me, kiss me for the last time.'* A romantic song."

"You are wrong. It is a political song."

"You are joking."

"No listen to the song, *'kiss me, kiss me for the last time.'* It is a revolutionary song. A revolutionary poet was imprisoned in Iran. The night before his hanging he was granted one last wish. He asked his guard for a pen and paper. He wrote a poem and requested the guard to smuggle it out of prison. The guard granted this final request of a dying man. The poet speaks to his beloved, who is also a revolutionary, to kiss him for the last time before his death. Later it became a famous song."

Silence broke between them. They both paid attention to the wording of the song. Hamid imagined a dark cold room where the poet had been imprisoned. His only crime had been his beliefs and yet, in the last moment of life he didn't forget his responsibility. He wrote a poem to remind his comrades not to forget the revolution and to never give up. There would be many lives sacrificed, but the final victory will be theirs.

Kiss me, kiss me
For the last time, goodbye to you, I am going to my destination
Our spring has passed, past is passed, and I am searching for my destination
Amidst the storm in a boat, having the same faith as the captain
Must sacrifice to pass the storm
In the middle of the night I am holding a promise with my friend
To light a fire in the mountains
I travel in the dark night, taking a dark path
My love, don't shed a tear of sorrow for me
Beautiful girl, I am your guest tonight, I stay with you so put your head on my shoulder

Nasrat lived alone. His mother had died two years ago and his older brother had gone to study at Moscow. His brother had not received a scholarship, but had been simply invited by the Communist party of the Soviet Union to study there. In fact, the invitation was just an excuse. He was there to become a good communist. Later Nasrat too went to Russia for studies and stayed with his older brother. When Nasrat finished his studies he returned to Afghanistan, but the communist party had asked his brother to stay on a bit longer in Moscow.

The living room was filled with books on wall-to-wall shelves. Hamid was excited to have a library so close to his home. Doctor Nasrat offered that he could come by any time to borrow a book.

"It is time for you to read what is necessary in becoming a communist comrade," Doctor Nasrat said.

"Really, this is a different world for me. I have never read Russian writers before and there are so many books," he said, overwhelmed by the shelves.

"Let me get you some tea," Nasrat said.

While Doctor Nasrat was in the kitchen, Hamid browsed through the titles of the books and read some of their back covers. He had never seen such abundance of books in one house and never imagined that a private Kabul resident could own so many. Other people frequented libraries for such access. Boys of Hamid's age did not spend time reading books, apart from what they were forced to read for school.

"Here is the tea," Doctor Nasrat offered.

"I am amazed by the number of books you have!" Hamid took a sip, tasting the cardamom in the tea.

"Comrade, you are most welcome to read any of them or borrow them, even if I am not here. I will leave a key with you."

"I could gain so much knowledge reading these books."

"Ha, but you have to be careful. Knowledge without practice is useless."

"But how can I practice by reading one of these books?"

"You have already joined the Communist party, that in itself is practical."

"You know that we have a proverb: *elm bay amal* is like a donkey carrying too many books."

"I know another one. *Khar eisa garash bam aka barand choon byayad hanooz khar bashad.*"

"Yes, if the donkey of Jesus goes to Mecca, when it returns it will still be a donkey."

"I don't want to be that donkey, Comrade"

Hamid spent hours discussing politics with Doctor Nasrat. When he was about to leave Doctor Nasrat lent him a book titled 'Dictionary of Political Words.'

"Comrade, I noticed how enthusiastic you were in using political vocabulary. But first you must learn their meaning."

Hamid went home, but returned a few days later to borrow

another book. He loved his visits to Nasrat's house; reading now became a part time habit, like a drug. How could he spend the long nights in Kabul without reading a book? Friendship between the two comrades became stronger. Under Nasrat's guidance, Hamid read books by many post Russian revolutionary poets and authors who were committed to communism. His favourites were Boris Pasternak and Chingiz Aimatov. Hamid did not have to wait until the Friday meetings. He could meet Nasrat, day and night. They would discuss books and politics and fly pigeons together. Hamid was painting his future in the vast canvas of the sky.

Meetings with Nasrat and the extensive reading had a great impact on Hamid and he changed from a romantic into a revolutionary poet. He wanted to be exactly like his other comrades, but in thinking only. For him to look like Vladimir Ilyich Lenin was not of such great importance. What was more so, was to carry the soul of this great man, and for Hamid this signified his communism. During the next months and years to come, Nasrat would capture many pigeons and lose others. Hamid would comfort his losses by saying that he would be the ultimate winner. At some point Nasrat found out that his brother had died in Moscow due to the pleasure of Russian women and excessive vodka. Hamid would replace his brother and become a comrade.

CHAPTER 5

The two girls were lying on their stomachs on *toshak,* reading their books and preparing themselves for the midterm exam when Roshan took her eyes away from her book and asked:

"Safa, what will you do after you finish school?"

"I will get married and have many children," Safa replied laughing.

"I don't believe you."

"Why not?"

"I know you will not stop studying and in two years time you will be in university. Girls like me have no chance of going to university and I am sure that my parents cannot wait to see me finish secondary school before marrying me to someone. It is a tradition in my family. All my cousins got married after secondary school and some girls were not even allowed to finish their schooling. Even if you don't want to go to university, your father would not simply let you marry."

"I don't know about that, Roshan, but now let's get back to our studies. Tell me how simple carbon can be changed into diamond? Remember we have a geology exam tomorrow."

Outside it was sunny. When it was like this the women of Andrabi knew that they would be extremely busy. They started the day with a thorough house cleaning. Using brooms made of bush, they cleaned each internal room before proceeding to the outdoor verandas and courtyard.

And if they thought that the carpets needed cleaning, for they were very meticulous, they would beat the dust off them using simple wooden sticks. These women needed to be strong to finish beating the carpets with the force of the Almighty before lunchtime. But that was not all; the next chore was to wash the clothes of the entire family in a clay pot that the master of the house had bought for traditional washing. On days like this Andrabi was full of all the world's colours: green, yellow, red, brown, blue, black *piran* and *tonban* local dress. A great variety of traditional colourful clothes were pegged on ropes extended across the walls of flat rooftops. It was on days like this that the undergarments of men and women were seen fluttering in the wind. Women frequently lent each other a helping hand with the heavy load of those chores.

Roya, one of the migrants from northern Afghanistan, accompanied by her daughter Safa went to help her neighbour Nasrin, mother of Roshan and Golo, with the washing. They had become good friends since Safa's family moved to Andrabi and had rented two rooms in Toftofi's house, owned by Roshan's father. Nasrin made no big deal of the class difference between the two families. Sometimes Nasrin returned the favour in helping to wash the clothes of Safa's family. Even the men of the two households became good friends. They often met each other at the mosque, as both families were God fearing, despite the funny nickname of Roshan's father, 'Toftofi' translated to 'the spitting man'. According to local gossip he was seen spitting on the palm of his hand and rubbing it on the lower part of his body one day. Nobody recalled specifically when he acquired that name, or how old he was, but behind his back, he was referred to by this nickname. Everyone addressed him to his face by his real name, Kaka Qadir. For Safa's family, as migrants from the north, mingling with their upper class friends, these rumours did not matter much. What mattered above all was that Roshan's family was God fearing and that Toftofi was the head of the family.

Toftofi's house was no ordinary house. It was probably the biggest house in Andrabi with its fourteen rooms built on two levels and a big central courtyard with apple and pear trees. The water came from the central well for washing and other chores. There was a small ceramic fishpond about five meters away from the well. Its ceramic tiles had come from Turkey many years ago. The courtyard was beautifully decorated with different types of flowers. The upper floor was surrounded with a meter and half of wooden verandas that were supported by carved wooden beams.

Each room was massive in size. The ceilings of the rooms were decorated with *mosata* or wooden artwork, which extended to another meter wide wooden fringe, all carved by artistically skilled carpenters. The window shutters were made of a unique walnut wood that opened elegantly by sliding. A special mechanism held the shutters at just the right level. The house was built by Toftofi's ancestor eleven generations before him and had already seen its glory days. The ancestor had been an important dignitary at the Mughal courts in the kingdom of Kabulistan. Toftofi was full of stories and legends of their ancestral home and the family's relationship with the court. He told stories of when the great Mughal King, Akbar, came to Kabul from India to visit the tomb of his grandfather Babur and gave the entire village of Andrabi to his ancestor in appreciation of his services.

No one could distinguish legend from history or how true Toftofi's stories really were. It was in the nature of the good people of Kabul to act important and relate themselves to kings. The fact remained that Toftofi would never move from his ancestral home to the modern parts of Kabul, as his brother had done. For him the glorious stories attached to their home were very important. The authentic house made people want to believe his stories. Toftofi enjoyed acting like a Mughal. He knew that if he moved to the modern part of the city, he would be among the many migrants to Kabul and that he would be not more important than them. In modern Kabul there would be no evidence of his ancestral ties to the Mughal court.

Roshan was curious about the stories Toftofi told and asked her mother one day while helping in the kitchen: "Are the stories I hear about our family true?"

"What stories are you talking about?"

"That we were once rich."

"That is true."

"Richer than all the people of Andrabi?"

"Yes."

"So what happened?"

"Your father, may Allah bless his soul, lost all his money."

"Lost all his money? How?"

"He was a gambler."

"Father is so God fearing. I can't imagine him gambling."

"Yes, he used to. It was Allah who saved us from poverty."

"Tell me mother jan, what happened?"

"Fifteen years ago your father was rich and wealthy with many properties. But alas, he lost much of his good fortune at the gambling tables. Each time he lost he gambled more to win his loss back. And when he won them back he gambled again because he couldn't stop. He was convinced that neither his luck nor his fortune would desert him, until one day he lost everything except his old and glorious ancestral home."

"Oh, God! Was he going to lose our home as well?"

"Yes. This is when I had to stop him."

"How did you do it?"

"One evening with tears in my eyes, I brought the Holy Koran, placed his hand on it and made him to swear that he would never gamble again. That was how he stopped and became a God fearing man who attended the mosque regularly."

"You are brave, mother."

"I didn't have a choice. I didn't want to see you all on the street, without a home."

"That must have helped father too."

"Yes. It was finally at a ripe old age, when he had no wealth and servants left that he found peace in his heart and decided not to let it go."

For Nasrin, living with less money was not a problem. She was happy, even if she had lost wealth, that she was able to save her husband and keep her house. After all, how many people in Kabul were owners of a house with fourteen rooms? The house itself was more than enough for four of them; husband, wife and two children. She had wanted more children, but God gave her only two. When the good people of Andrabi, many of whom had a minimum of eight children, asked her why she had only two, she replied with laughter that her husband had spent most of his nights gambling and had not always performed his duty as a husband.

On this warm day Nasrin was in the centre of the courtyard, not far from the well that provided her with cold water. Hot water was carried from inside the house. In front of her stood her family's clay pot and another clay pot was set in front of Roya. The two women busily washed their clothes and chatted with each other. There was no sign of the servants that the Roshan family had employed before. Time had come for Nasrin to do her own chores and she did not mind.

Meanwhile Roshan and Safa were in Roshan's room chatting and studying. They were in the same school and in the same class. They only had one difference: they didn't have the same talent. Safa was the top student of her class and Roshan needed her friendship and support to pass her exams. The reason for Safa's excellence was the help of her father. He was a highly educated man with a degree in history. He had graduated from Kabul University and secured himself a teaching job in one of the best high schools of the city. When he got the job he brought his family to Kabul with him. During the day he taught his pupils with much dedication and in the evening he helped his daughter with her schoolwork, always keeping her one or two steps ahead of her classmates. He not only taught his daughter the normal school books, but went beyond that: introducing her to great literature and making sure that she read the newspaper and was aware of the current affairs of the world. Safa was sometimes even ahead of her teachers and that was one of the reasons that she was not liked by all of them.

They were busy studying when a knock on the door interrupted them and Golo entered, apologising. He needed to borrow his sister's math book. Golo and Roshan were twins and studied at the same level. After Golo left, the two girls looked into each other's eyes and shared a meaningful laugh. Those days Golo made various excuses to enter Roshan's room when he knew that Safa was there.

"I'm burning. This place is so hot," Roshan jumped up and leant out of the window to catch some fresh air. Safa joined her.

"You said you wanted to study and didn't want to be disturbed," Roshan said.

"Yes Bibi jan that was my plan. If there was a bit more incoming breeze, I could breathe more easily. You're blocking it."

"Don't Bibi jan me madam, I see that the heat of the exams is getting to you. You're feeling nervous. Competition, competition. You don't want to lose your status in class."

"I'm not worried about competition and I'm not feeling nervous either."

"Do you think my brother looked nervous as well?"

"Why? Because he's worried that he'd lose his status?"

"No he is not as brainy as you."

"Ha, ha, ha, very funny!"

"With my parents on his side, Golo can't go wrong. I'm sure he will always be just as important as he is right now, even if he were to fail all his exams."

"Aha Bibi jan I can see there's a hint of jealousy in your voice."

"I'm not jealous. Let's go down to the courtyard; it is cooler there," she suggested.

"I can't Roshan. But if you want to, you can go. I must return."

"No, no please stay," she pleaded.

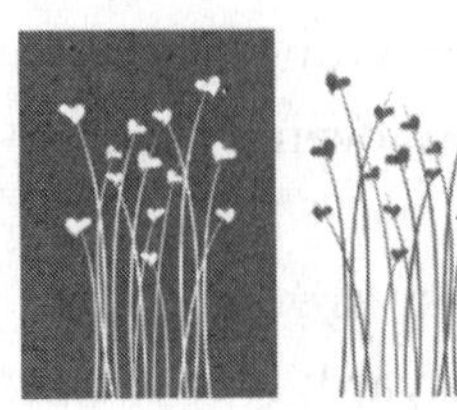

CHAPTER 6

"Oh! How cold it is here. I can't believe it. In the city I was dying of the heat and was looking for shades to catch fresh air and now here I am sure that I will not be able to sleep without having a big blanket on me tonight," Golo said with his hand crossed against his chest.

"Yes and it is less than an hour's drive from the city," Hamid said.

"Look at that house," Golo pointed to a modern concrete building, made tastefully.

"That is the house of Ahmad Zahir, our famous musician. Most of the weekends, he plays music for his friends in that house. His friends come here with their girlfriends. They listen to music, they dance and drink wine."

"How do you know?"

"I come here with my family in the weekend and spend a night in the house of one of our relatives whose family has moved to America. I tell you at night the voice of Ahmad Zahir echoes in these beautiful mountains. We hear the sound of their laughter. That is life my friend; women, wine and music. And in daylight we see them walking around; men and women holding hands, enjoying the cold weather."

"That is the beauty of Kabul. It is summer and winter at the same time," Hamid said.

"You and your poetic description."

"The best description of Kabul is done in Tozok-e Babury."

"What is that?"

"Surely you know that. You learned about Babur at school. He was the King of Kabul. He loved this place and said: "At a day's distance from Kabul one is in the heat of summer and half a day away one can see the snow capped mountains."

"*Bachaim,* who cares about Babur! It is more important to enjoy life. He may have written about it, but I enjoy Kabul practically. I walk in this beautiful place, I swim in the river, I eat its delicious fruit, I see its beautiful flowers."

"Golo, you missed the point. And please don't call me your son."

"OK *Bachaim,* I promise. But since we speak of writing, you need to write me another letter to my beloved."

"You idiot, if you had read Babur at school as you should have, you could have written the letters by yourself!"

"And who would have brought you here, to this idyllic place? You write and I discover wonderful places and get inspired by them. Life has given us different purposes. You are the poet and I am the provider!"

"I am tired of your stupid jokes."

"Hamid, you are over sensitive."

"And you are simply stupid."

"Every poet needs a stupid counterperson."

"I agree!"

Hamid and Golo had been friends since childhood. They lived in Andrabi, went to the same school, but were not in the same class. Their friendship began without purpose and survived the same way. It was Golo who first asked Hamid to join him and enjoy beautiful places in each other's company. Later when Golo fell in love, he used Hamid's talent in writing love letters. Although Hamid and Golo had no secrets, he did not speak of his love for a girl, which was unacceptable in their society. Hamid knew the rules and did not push his friend to tell him whom he loved. It was better for both of them. Hamid also did not wish to get involved. In a way the situation suited him. They visited beautiful places and escaping the heat inspired him to write. Sometimes when he wrote love letters for Golo, he imagined that he was writing to his own beloved.

My Heart, I did not imagine that my sorrows would deepen when you accepted my love. I am sitting here in Paghman, the place which Babur the poet described so well. Its beauty has no comparison and yet I am lonely. I read his poems and think of you. I wish I could share his descriptions with you. You must have heard of him. I imagine you here among the abundance of tulips that he described. Nothing has changed since Babur wrote about this place 500 years ago. Maybe its beauty is even more magnificent today.

He maintained that life was short and to be enjoyed. He was right. The man who conquered almost all of India is now dead. The legacy he left for us was his love for beauty. You are so beautiful. I wish I was a poet like Babur to describe your beauty. My heart is a garden and your love is the most beautiful flower growing in me. Babur's quoted Hafiz, his favourite poet:
'Rose petals let us scatter
And fill the cup with red wine
The firmaments let us shatter
And come with a new design'
But I personally prefer his other poem:
'Flowers of this garden will not remain fresh forever
Accept my love, when you are still capable of loving'
There is no doubt that you cannot remain indifferent towards my love for you. But please don't wait too long and regret will not bring any good

They sat under the shade of a chenar tree. A breeze that blew from the top of the ice-capped mountains was bringing a gust of cool air. Kabul River was only 100 meters away. Hamid read the letter that he had written out loud. Soon after, Golo stripped off his clothes down to his underwear.

"Brother your award for writing such a romantic letter is to jump into the river."

Hamid did not jump.

"You aren't wearing underwear?"

"No, I don't know how to swim."

"Learn to swim, brother! I am not a poet but I know how to swim."

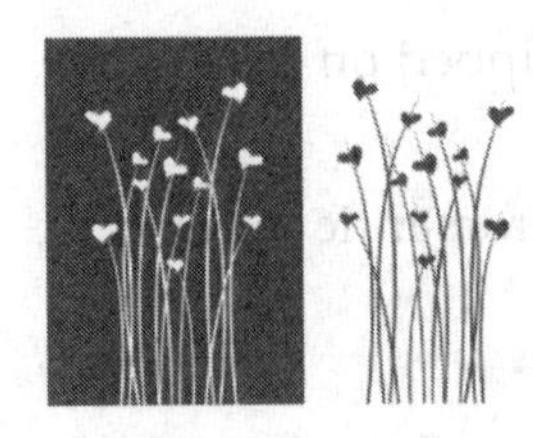

CHAPTER 7

"Hey, if you really want to enjoy washing yourself you must go to the hamam," Safa said without thinking. The idea suddenly came to Safa one day when she was at Roshan's house. Roshan had just come out of the bathroom after a shower with a towel wrapped around her head.

"Aha, that is a forbidden area for me," Roshan said.

"Why, because you are too posh?"

"Don't be silly. I can't go because my mother doesn't want me to go to such places and I cannot go alone."

"And why doesn't your mother want you to go?"

"Oh Safa, you ask too many questions. But if you want to know, she says that she doesn't like public baths."

"I see. So she is posh."

"Safa, please give it up. No one is posh in our house."

"Prove it then."

"What do you mean?"

"Come with me to the hamam."

"I told you, mother would not allow me."

"She won't allow you to go alone but if you come with me she will accept."

"I am not sure."

"Leave it to me. I will talk to your mother."

"Oh you angel from Nijrab. Only you could influence my mother, because you can't do anything wrong. You are an angel."

"Stop being sarcastic. Tell me if you want to go or not. I am telling you it would be great fun."

"And you promise to talk with my mother. In that case I am always ready for an adventure. In this country there is nothing for women apart from going to the hamam or to that ridiculous park reserved for women."

A week later, when the light of the day had not yet spread its wings, Roshan and Safa were walking carefully, making sure not to fall in a pothole or hit a stone or any other object that would make them trip. They walked narrow streets to reach the hamam. They had gotten up with the *azan* of the mullah and without wasting any time, took the bags they had prepared the night before and left. Safa was in the courtyard first and a few minutes later Roshan appeared. Leaving home so early was a new adventure for them and walking in the streets with sleepy eyes proved to be difficult. They had everything they needed for the hamam in their bags. Both mothers had helped them to pack. They had towels to dry themselves after washing, as well as a black honeycombed stone to scrape the soles of their feet, *leef* or a body scraper, *kisa* a second body scraper, *gel-e sar shoy* brown mud for the hair, *rooi shoya* white mud for the face, soap, shampoo, small containers for water and clean clothes to replace their used ones.

For the girls, it was a double triumph: they celebrated their independence on the day their country was celebrating Independence Day as well. It was a public holiday. For the first time they were away from the house, going to a public bath without being accompanied by their mothers. Roshan never had been to a hamam before and she did not really have the need to go to such places. In her house there were nice bathrooms and she could wash herself wherever she fancied.

The walk had taken less than 10 minutes. When they came to the entrance of the hamam they headed for a small door, only wide enough for one woman to pass through at a time. As soon as Roshan entered the heat hit her face.

"Better get used to it," Safa warned. "This is only the entrance hall. Inside is much hotter, but I'm sure you'll love it."

"May you suffer from heat of hell Safa for bringing me here," Roshan laughed.

"Come in, don't block the entrance," The ugly woman shouted from behind the counter where she collected money. She had yellow teeth, from smoking *chilim.*

"Don't shout, we are coming," Safa responded to the angry tone.

"Listen madam, you have to use your brain. You and your friend are standing at the entrance, blocking the way for people to get in and out."

"Okay, okay. How much is it to get in?"

"Is it your first time? You should know how much it is. Nothing has changed," the woman said impatiently.

Safa saw that Roshan was uncomfortable. "Don't worry Roshan, these women always act like this," she whispered. "They must sound tough and impolite to control women. They are harmless." She put the money down on the counter and paid for both of them.

Just then, a woman entered with three children: two girls and a young boy. The woman behind the counter switched her attention to her new customers and shouted: "You should have brought the boy's father as well!"

"He is less than six years old. Okay, next time I will bring his father too," the new customer said.

"He looks more than six to me."

"Look, he is not circumcised yet. Trust me he is only six years old."

"I don't want to see his body. This is the last time and I mean it."

"You are harsh, Nazo. I am a regular customer."

"Regular or not regular, rules are rules. I can't allow young men in here. It will damage our reputation. This place is for women and very young children only. Look at your boy, how he is looking at the women."

The poor boy was looking around scared, not because he was interested in observing women's bodies, but because he was embarrassed and shocked by the argument.

The women changed their clothes in the entrance hall. Both Safa and Roshan started undressing. Roshan felt like the small boy looking at everything. She had to be careful, she did not want to break the rules and be accused of doing something wrong on her first visit. Yet she was fascinated and inquisitive. Someone brought them two *lungs.* Safa helped Roshan put it on. It was like a large towel to wrap it around their body while washing. It covered from breast downwards to the knee. Safa explained that this piece of cloth was only symbolic. Sometimes the women inside the hamam would take the *lung* off to pour water over themselves or when they were being massaged by a hamam attendant. There were plenty of hamam attendants for massages and Safa suggested that they must have one as well.

"There is no way that I will show my body here," Roshan protested.

"No one will be interested to see your body, silly. Everyone is busy scraping the dirt and dry skin from their body. Looking at you will be waste of time. They need to go back home to deliver their clean bodies to their husbands, who are waiting for them," Safa joked.

"Ha, ha, ha, you idiot."

They went inside the hamam and the noise of the place hit them. It was dark everywhere. The only place that was providing a bit of light was at the top of the dome where a circled glass was placed to provide light and to keep away snow and rain. It took some time for their eyes to get used to the place. They finally saw some benches at the edge of the hamam for the women to sit on. There was very little space left on benches, but they managed to sit in a corner not far from the two huge stone containers that provided hot and cold water for washing. Women gathered around containers, splashing water on themselves. Some women were lying on the floor with their relatives or hamam attendants scrubbing their backs and giving them massage or getting the dirty skin off their body. As soon as they sat, Safa took the initiative and brought hot water to Roshan, threw it on her body and started to scrape her back. A while later the daylight reached the top of the dome where the glass was. Now they could see each other. Roshan slowly got used to the place, brought water, threw it on Safa and began scraping her back while continuing to look around. She was impressed to see women lying on the floor completely naked with a hamam attendant on top massaging them.

The *lung* or the piece of cloth that was provided by the hamam was as good as having nothing on, because as soon as it became wet, it revealed the woman's every curve. Everything became visible in a more poetic way, apart from the private parts, which were left to the imagination. There were all types of women: ugly, fat and slim women. The amazing thing was that they all looked at each other, evaluating each other's beauty.

The women would soak up a big chunk of *gel-e sar shoy* in a small pot and then dissolve it in the copper *lagan* by rubbing it against the smooth finish that turned it into a thick paste. They would apply this to their hair like shampoo and then rinse it off with warm water. One could smell a combination of humidity, sweat and aromatic soaps.

A woman tripped over someone who was lying on the floor, and fell.

"You kicked me," the woman on the floor yelled.

"Well, it's a stupid place to lie there."

"Are you blind?"

"No, I am not blind, but I didn't know that you could spread your legs so wide apart."

"Don't talk to me like that, you whore!"

"Go away you *kanchani*. Last night you were fucked by all men of Kabul and today you are here to wash your filth."

"Wa, wa, wa. Aren't you the one who was kicked out of the house by her husband, because you were caught with a donkey on top of you?"

"No, I am the one who saw men marching towards your cunt. It was just behind the hamam during the day. I was the one who saw your filthy cunt open, open and open like a tunnel and invite men inside. Remember?"

The laughter and jeering of the others encouraged the two women to continue their row. Warmed by their audience, they continued to shout new accusations. Roshan was fascinated; she thought it was incredible fun to be there.

The two girls were busy helping each other wash when Roshan saw a middle age woman coming towards her. Her heart sank, worried that she had done something wrong and the woman was coming to pick a fight with her.

"Are you Roshan?" the woman asked.

"Yes," Roshan replied.

"Don't you remember me, you silly girl? I am your aunt. I have been to your house many times. How are you?"

"*Salam* aunt. Sorry, it is very dark here and I could not see your face properly."

"Oh, never mind. How is your mother? How is your father? And how is Golo?"

"They are fine. I came with my friend to the hamam for the first time," Roshan replied, looking at Safa.

"Salam. Yes, I insisted that she should come here," Safa said.

"I am glad that you did that. Otherwise I was going to forget the face of this angel," the woman said. "You know this naughty girl may not remember but I am her mother's best friend and I have been to their house for lunch and dinner many times. Of course at that time this *naznin* was only a small child."

Roshan was clearly embarrassed, hoping that the woman could not go on talking about her childhood. Normally rude people would say: you don't remember, but when you were small I cleaned your shit. But the woman did not follow that thread of conversation.

"Yes, I see that you are new here and don't know how to wash. Let me rub your back."

"No, no aunt, I don't want to trouble you," Roshan begged.

"Nonsense girl, don't be shy with me. I have seen all of you before."

Roshan realised that the woman would talk about her childhood and embarrass her in front of Safa. So she let the woman work on her with the *leef* in her hand, scraping the dry skin off her back. Seniority was very important in Afghanistan and elderly people frequently used this power on younger people. The young who did not follow this rule were labelled as impolite. Roshan had never been impolite to an older person. Despite her displeasure she let the woman continue rubbing her back. When she left Roshan even managed to thank her, not only once, but ten times, as it was the custom in the country. Cleaning Roshan took a long time and perhaps the woman enjoyed being helpful. When she was done she told Roshan that she looked like a princess, and if she went to any house she would be the light of that house and she wished that would be her house.

When the woman left Safa asked, "Was she really your aunt?"

"Don't act as if you are stupid. In this country every man who is older than us is our uncle and every woman is older than us is our aunt. You know that."

"Of course I know, but no artificial aunt of mine ever came to rub my back. Are you sure this is not your real aunt?"

"Yes, she is. This aunt came to our house when I was little, so I can't remember her. After that she disappeared," Safa said impatiently.

"Sorry, I was just teasing you. But you must admit that this woman is not a typical aunt or she has something in mind."

"What in mind?"

"Well, I don't know, perhaps she and your mother broke their friendship many years ago and now that she saw you again she wants to renew her friendship. Did you notice that she mentioned coming to your house again?"

Later the two girls went to the changing area and put on clean clothes. But before that Safa rubbed olive oil on Roshan's body and Roshan did the same for Safa. Now the two women with smooth warm bodies were back on the street heading to their homes. They had none to deliver their bodies to, since they had no husbands. Was it good to remain without a husband and enjoy a single life or to have a husband and wash your body for him to feel your warm skin? Time would tell.

It was late morning and the sun was shining. Some of the shops were closed and some were open. There were not many pedestrians on the streets because of Independence Day. Most of the shops would open again in the evening when people poured onto the streets to go to *chaman,* where there would be fireworks and entertainment with music being played in camps that were built for this purpose.

"So how was it?" Safa asked.

"How was what? Oh you mean the hamam."

"Of course, you absent minded queen."

"I don't know what to say. It was scary but also fun."

"Most scary things are fun."

"Like?"

"Like being kissed before marriage. You like it and yet you are scared because if you get caught you will be punished and pay for the rest of your life."

"I think the water in the hamam went to your head."

"Do you want to hear about fun and fear in the *hamam*?"

"Again, you and your stories."

"Do you want to?"

"Okay, go on then, at least I will forget my hunger. I am so hungry. We stayed there for a very long time."

Many, many years ago there was a man who looked very feminine, with no hair on his face or legs; he even had small breasts. His name was Noso and he worked as a masseur in a special hamam where the daughters and wives of rich and influential people, including the daughter of the wazir, came.

Noso was very happy giving massages to rich women and touching their bodies. He also realised that some women really enjoyed massages from him and asked him to go further and touch the parts that were normally kept for husbands only. Of course, they didn't know that he was a man. Almost every woman asked for him saying that her touch was special. Noso really touched them with care, a touch that was enjoyable for both. But one day calamity struck the hamam. The most expensive jewel of the daughter of the wazir had disappeared. The women in charge of the hamam searched everywhere, but could not find it. They went through every woman's belongings and still could not find it.

Finally, they decided to strip down and search each woman, one by one, taking their lung away. Noso almost died of fright. He shook with fear and knew that the time had come for him to reveal his identity to the king and for his sins he would immediately be killed. He began to pray in his heart and promised Allah if his life was saved he would never do anything like this again. At that moment he fainted. All the women were frantic by this new incident and their attention was now directed to him. At the same time the real thief found an opportunity to leave the jewel somewhere that would be seen without knowing who had left it there. The jewel had been found. A few minutes later Noso opened his eyes and left the hamam, never to return again.

"What a story!" Roshan said

"Yes, the hamam has many stories."

"Do you think there was a Noso in the *hamam* today?"

"Yes, sure, it was your aunt. Did you notice how she enjoyed touching you?"

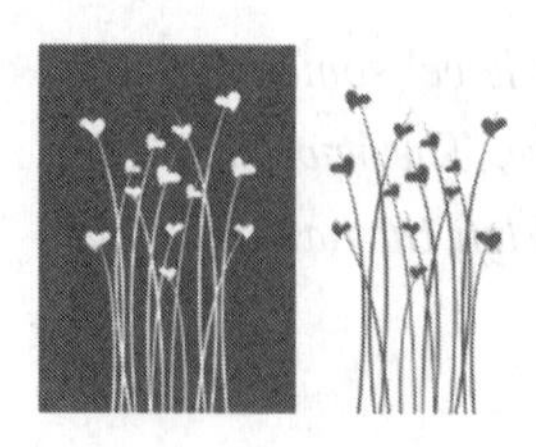

CHAPTER 8

The mosque was the focus for community involvement and Rabani was the centre. After prayers he could be found in a quiet corner of the mosque whispering. People thought that the mullah was eccentric. In fact, Rabani did not waste his time in conversation with the local worshipers, mostly uneducated and ignorant. He preferred to have a direct conversation with God. He asked questions and God was generous to give him answers. Suffering during his childhood, the knowledge he gained in India, the loss of his family and finally his arrival at Andrabi, were all planned by God. He kept reciting the Koran and it gave him guidance.

Blessed is He in whose hands is the Kingdom – who is powerful over everything – who has created life and death, so that He might test which amongst you conducts himself well.

Life was a test for him, a narrow bridge that he had to cross, trying hard not to fall. To fall was to welcome confusion, rejection, not obeying God, falling into Hell.

I seek refuge in the Lord of the people. The King of the people. The God of the people. From the evils of sneaky whisperers. Who whisper into the chests of the people. Be they of the jinns, or the people.

Not everything was as beautiful, as simple and as innocent as love. Mullah Rabani was complicated. He had become this way because of the way life had treated him. In each line of his face was a mark of his history and each hair of his beard could tell another story. He came to Andrabi in a mysterious way. Now he lived in the mosque, the place where worshipers declared their unconditional love to God. Before coming here he had already travelled to countries outside Afghanistan and had seen much more than ordinary people of Kabul who were only familiar with their own city. His journey began when he was just a child.

As one of his best students, Rahmat knew many of the details of Rabani's childhood and youth. One day he was sitting in front of Rabani with the Koran wide open when Rahmat noticed that the eyes of mullah had drifted away and he was no longer present. Rahmat closed the Koran and deliberated long whether he should ask the question that he had always wanted to. "Excuse me, Mullah Sahib! Why did you go to Deoband in India to learn about Islam?" As soon as Rahmat asked this question, he immediately felt he ought not to have done so. Yet he was curious about his teacher, this man of Islam, with his incredible knowledge, who had gone all the way to India to gain it.

"It's a sad story," Rabani smiled, stroking his beard to divert his attention away from the question. But now that Rahmat had had the courage to ask the question, he was not going to give up so easily.

"How can it be sad when you have acquired so much knowledge?"

"I see that you are insisting. It really is a sad story."

"Please tell me, Mullah Sahib!"

"Why do you want to know?"

"I like learning from you. I respect you tremendously. It makes me determined to learn even more about Islam."

"Going to India was not my choice. It just happened."

"What happened then?"

"Talking about it brings back sad memories."

"Were you thinking about it, a moment ago, when you drifted away?"

"Yes I was remembering the day when I was for sale on the streets of Kabul."

"What?"

"It was after we came to Kabul. My mother died. My father had lost all his crops due to drought. So he brought us, me and my two sisters, to Kabul in the hope of finding a job. We were not the only family in such circumstances. Almost everyone from the Northern provinces had travelled to Kabul in search of food and shelter but the city didn't provide either. People ate food from the garbage bins; they slept out in the streets. Parents witnessed their children dying of hunger. They were scared. They offered their children to the Kabulis to buy them. But the God fearing people of Kabul were only interested in buying girls. My two sisters were given away to two men. My father was desperate. He tried to make enquiries about the men who took my sisters. But how could he be sure? Otherwise, my sisters would have starved to death. He was torn apart. And I? He had no other choice but to send me with a mullah to Deoband, India to become a student of a madrasa. That was how I learned the Koran and escaped from death.

"Oh merciful Allah," Rahmat was indeed shocked.

"I'll tell you the rest of the story some other time. Right now it's *namaz* and I must go for ablutions." Rabani got up. Rahmat kissed his book as a mark of respect, covered it with a rich green cloth, smelling of rose water, and replaced it carefully on one of the shelves. He left the mosque quietly, pensively, and returned home for ablutions.

Rabani thought about telling the rest of his story to Rahmat the following day, but finally settled for other stories to instruct him. These were the stories of the prophet and his disciples, who throughout hardship had unwaveringly continued to spread the word of Allah. Rabani thought that these stories would inspire Rahmat.

Life had prepared Rabani to become one of the elites among the mullahs of Afghanistan. While other mullahs were struggling with one language, Rabani spoke Farsi, Urdu and Arabic fluently. The madrasa in Deoband offered the best for Islamic studies and his knowledge was much deeper than the education offered by other schools. He also learned Greek philosophy and Hinduism. He knew the entire Koran by heart and could quote any verse from it.

Life was not easy in India. The madrasa had strict rules such as waking up much earlier than *azan,* the call for prayers, having to prepare water for his teachers for ablution, cleaning the mosque, preparing breakfast for teachers and students, studying Islamic subjects after morning prayers and going from house to house to collect alms for the madrasa. All the students were requested to do this. Harsh life had robbed him of a sweet childhood. Rules for learning were very unforgiving and most of the time the teachers beat him for not learning fast enough or for making mistakes. He and his friends never smiled, never laughed. It was considered to be disrespectful to the teachers. No one encouraged the children to play.

As he grew up he learned about The kingdom of Islam: there was only one kingdom and that was the kingdom of God. All Muslims were brothers and had to undertake *jihad* to create the one and only kingdom of God. This was his *farz,* his duty. He strongly believed this doctrine and put his belief into practice in 1971. It was the year when the third war between India and Pakistan broke out and he took up arms to fight on the side of the Pakistani Muslims. Many young men did the same and most did not make it, but Rabani was lucky and survived the war. After the war he stayed in Pakistan. It was no longer safe for him to return to India, since he was considered an enemy for siding with Pakistan.

Rabani was now a man with ambition and knowledge and was soon called upon to work as a teacher in a Pakistani madrasa, where he became very popular with his students. But one day news came about his family and his country. Someone had seen his father many years ago begging on the streets of Kabul and said that he was in poor health. At that moment Rabani realized that he had a country of his own, where his family lived. One night he had an awful dream. His sick father was dying and asked him to come back to arrange his funeral.

He decided to leave Pakistan at once and go back to the place where he was born. Religion was very important to him, but his family was important too. Islam said that heaven was under the feet of parents and yet he had not been in touch with his father and his sisters in years. Where were they? He had reasons for not returning home when he was a student in the Indian madrasa. His father had told him not to return until he had become a real scholar in Islamic studies. The other reason was not having any money. But now he was a respected teacher with a modest salary that could get him to get back to his native land, find his father and help out the family. He was not scared any more that he would not find a job in Afghanistan. Life had taught him that he could create possibilities out of nothing.

When he arrived home, he realized that nobody knew the whereabouts of his sisters and father in Kabul. After a long and fruitless search he decided to head towards his village in Badakhshan. There he found his father, buried under two meters of soil, dead for more than five years. Someone in the village had informed him that his father had never found the daughters he had sold in Kabul. The men who had bought the girls had disappeared. There was nothing left for Rabani in his village, apart from memories of hard times. He decided to return to Kabul.

Mullah Rabani had no trouble finding a job in a mosque. The mosque happened to be in Andrabi, where the previous mullah had recently passed away. The community was looking for a mullah with a great depth of knowledge of Islam and was enthusiastic to discover that Rabani was no ordinary mullah. He was a graduate of Deoband and not many mullahs in Kabul could match his credentials. What they didn't know was that Rabani believed in one world under the banner of Islam. Only Rahmat knew that they were appointing a mullah driven by a compulsive duty to campaign for Islam in his home country.

The mosque in Andrabi was designed for Friday prayers with a magnificent dome, wide windows towards the street, big columns supporting the roof and chandeliers hanging from the ceiling. In summer worshipers used the veranda when the interior of the mosque was too full to hold everyone. Sometimes they even spread their prayer mats on the road and blocked the people passing by. No one dared question the worshipers' rights to block the traffic. On Fridays, Andrabi and its surroundings stood still and listened in silence to Rabani's voice issued from the loudspeaker of the minaret. When he quoted a verse his voice became melodious and one had to shut his eyes and listen to him with his heart. *O ye that believe! fear Allah and believe in His apostle and He will bestow on you a double portion of His Mercy: He will provide for you a light by which ye shall walk straight in your path and He will forgive your past: For Allah is Oft-Forgiving. Most Merciful.*

The mosque of Andrabi was one of the first mosques to use loudspeakers for Friday prayers and the government permitted it. Yet Rabani criticised the government for its lack of interest in Islam. He also criticised the Afghans for their low morals. "Women should not appear like this on the street, wearing western clothes. One can see their bodies. They do not wear the *hijab* and look at their faces, painted like dolls. Brothers, you will all go to hell because of your wives and sisters. Brothers, the Day of Judgment is not far and the torture of the grave is unbearable. My brothers, your wives and daughters should stay at home! They should leave the house only twice: once when they get married and the second time when they die."

The worshipers listened to Rabani. Deep in their hearts they wanted to take control and ask their wives and daughters to stay at home, but it was practically impossible. Girls went to school those days and wives worked either in offices or as teachers. Women continued to go out, and what Rabani preached created tension between family members. The Muslims of Andrabi were torn between modernism and tradition. They wanted to be modern and also keep the old tradition in line with Islam and that was impossible. They were not against their wives going to work in offices to bring extra money home for the family and yet they did not like to lose control. They wanted their daughters to go to school, but at the same time they worried that their education might influence them to free themselves from tradition.

For Rabani the biggest threat to Islam was modern education. He believed only in one type of education, like the one provided in madrasas like Deoband. In his speeches he tried to create fear in the hearts of people. He argued that the disappearance of young girls was related to modern education. A girl in her final studies in school fell in love with someone. The families had met but the girl's parents opposed her marriage. The young man had sent his parents many times to the house of the girl asking for her hand in marriage but they refused. They wanted her to marry someone who had the same status as her family. Finally the girl, influenced by her lover, ran away with him and disappeared one morning on her way to school. Rabani mentioned that incident again and again, trying to create fear in the fathers' minds, saying that this would happen if they sent their daughters to school. Some people really worried, not realising that there were already plenty of incidents like this happening in the rural areas of the country where there was no education. Rural girls not going to school often eloped. Rabani also said that it was not acceptable for honourable men to send their wives to work in offices where other men worked.

Rahmat was deeply attracted by Rabani's teaching. He was a teenager when Rabani became the mullah of Andrabi. From the start, Rabani impressed Rahmat. He was not like other mullahs of Afghanistan, who only knew a limited number of Islamic books and concentrated on leading *namaz*. He developed a great respect for this learned man, who had survived the drought and made the pilgrimage to India, graduated from the best Islamic institution and had fought on the side of fellow Muslims. Rahmat wanted to learn more than the basic philosophy of Islam and Rabani was there to teach him. In fact, Rabani became famous among many young Afghan Muslims and his mosque was packed with loyal followers. He captured the hearts of people he intended to help out: the young people of Andrabi and the nearby dwellings. They were educated and Rabani found them to be the right pupils.

During his *namaz* address he talked about Islam, politics of the time and of course about an Islamic movement called The Muslim Brotherhood (*Ikhwanul Muslimin*), which had been established in Egypt.

Rabani had big plans for Rahmat. One day Rabani would start his fight to create a kingdom of Allah and Rahmat would be his commander.

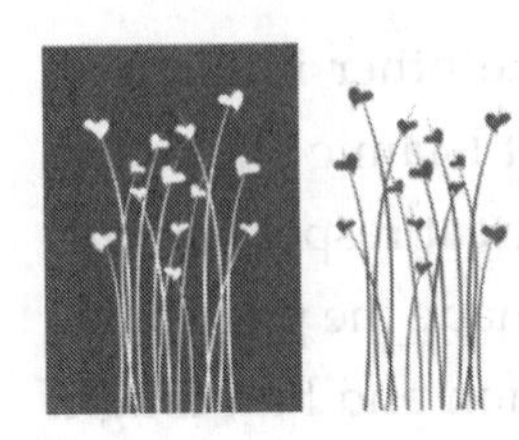

CHAPTER 9

"Allah, have a mercy on my soul."

Minutes ago Rabani was caught stealing from a bakery. The baker called the police and without showing any sympathy that he had only stolen a loaf of bread, the police held him tightly by the wrist, pulling him towards the police station. He cried and asked the onlookers for help, shouting for his father; but his father was not around and the onlookers just looked at him without interfering with the police. Sweat poured under his clothes when he woke up from the nightmare. Rabani frequently had nightmares associated with the awful drought, related to the year when he, his sisters and father were on the streets of Kabul, begging for food and shelter. Each time he remembered the nightmare, he began to shake uncomfortably.

It was afternoon, time between two *namaz*. The noon namaz had passed and the afternoon one would soon come. It was not the usual time for Rabani to sleep, but he was tired because he had been reading a new book by Sayyed Qutb throughout the night. The Egyptian writer's views on the role of Islam in the social and political arena were widely known. Rabani was first introduced to books written by Sayyed Qutb, while he was studying in India. He got up from his bed to go for ablution and to do some *nafil namaz*. These days he prayed less, but studied more about the work of scholars such as Sayyed Qutb, who shaped modern Islam in Egypt and its neighbouring countries but was still relatively unknown in Afghanistan. Qutb's philosophy appeared to him even when he was praying.

After *nafil* prayer there was a knock on the door of his room. Rabani never answered these knocks because most of the time he was busy reading books or praying. But this person insisted. It was Rahmat who had come for his Islamic studies.

"Asalam alaikom Mullah Sahib," Rahmat greeted Rabani.

"Walikom salam. Come and sit."

Rahmat sat in front of Rabani, opened his Koran holder, made with beautifully carved wood. Rahmat did not lay the Koran on it, but another book called *Fiqh in Islam*.

"You are almost at the end of this book," Rabani said.

"Yes," Rahmat replied.

"Rahmat, reading books in the dogmatic way will not give you in-depth knowledge. Have you understood *Fiqh in Islam*?"

"I think so."

"So you would be able to quote this book whenever you are trying to establish an argument in line with Islam?"

"I have read this book again and again and I assure you, Mullah Sahib, that I can remember almost every sentence."

"That is exactly what you shouldn't have done."

Rahmat was shocked by Rabani's paradox. The book, the philosophy of Islam, was recommended to him by Rabani and now Rabani was saying that he should not have memorised it.

"Don't look so shocked. What you have read and heard was the interpretation of Islam through this book and myself. The time has come to have your own interpretation. You must challenge me and challenge the author of this book. There must be issues that you do not agree with."

"I am not familiar with this kind of teaching. In school we are told to never question our teacher's lectures."

"And that is the reason that people don't know about Islam in Afghanistan, because we don't have good teachers. You must ask,

Rahmat. Question me, challenge me and challenge my books. Only that way you will have in-depth knowledge. Now we will open our first challenge. I will challenge your knowledge first. What is the ultimate goal for men like you and me?"

Rahmat was not ready for this type of conversation. Had he done something wrong? He thought about the question and tried to find the best answer.

"I think our goal is to understand Islam better."

Rabani smiled and replied. "It is an acceptable answer, but can't you think of anything else?"

"No, I can't."

"Our ultimate goal is to find the truth. On the way in finding the ultimate truth, we may find many truths, which will help us to reach our final goal."

"What do you mean by many truths?"

"For example, the truth behind the philosophy of the writer you are reading. Do we accept his truth or not? If we accept his truth, would that become our truth? If we don't accept his truth, that will also be our truth. That means our truth will be different from his truth and yet the book helps us to find our own truth."

Silence broke the discussion. Rahmat went in deep thought and Rabani sensed that.

"There was a man who died; no he was actually killed in Egypt many years ago, before you were born."

"Why was he killed and who was he?"

"He was killed by the government for defending his truth. His name was Sayyed Qutb."

"What did he do?"

"He searched for the truth. He challenged the Imams and other Islamic scholars of his time. He realised that their knowledge was not expanding and limited to quotations from The Koran. He wrote books. Imams did not like him, but that did not stop him even when he was accused of being lost and showing the wrong path to the followers of Islam."

"Do you believe in his truth?"

"Well, that is a good question. I have read his books. I challenge his truth to find my own. But his books have helped me to reach my final goal."

"What is your final goal or ultimate truth?"

"There is only one God and that is Allah. There is only one kingdom and that is Allah's kingdom and I will fight for it until my last breath."

"Today you have taught me different things, Mullah Sahib."

"You have been my student for many years. Today, I thought it was time for you to start learning new things."

"I found the discussion enjoyable."

"Learning becomes enjoyable when you are part of learning and teaching."

"I don't understand."

"I am learning from you when I am teaching you."

"I am so humble, Mullah Sahib. What can I teach you?"

"You teach me a great deal."

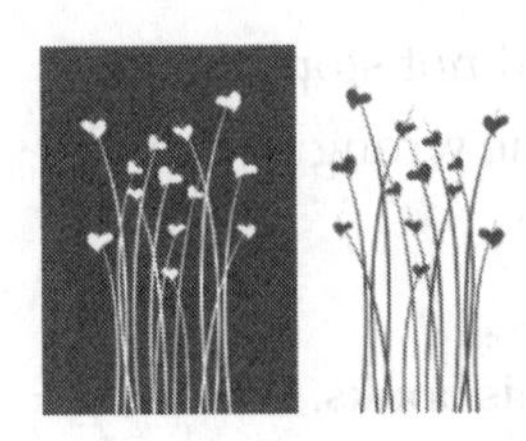

CHAPTER 10

A foreigner had entered the mosque much earlier than the midday prayer time and sat down in a corner. It was the end of autumn. As the weather got colder people began buying wood and coal to keep their houses warm. In the mosque, the *khadem* the keeper of the mosque, was storing wood for the stove and noticed the stranger, perhaps in his forties. Afghanistan had a history of foreign visitors. In those days there were two different types of visitors. The first type was the westerners who stayed in Kabul en route to India, breaking their journey by visiting several provinces of natural beauty and historical importance such as the Buddhas of Bamian and Band-e Amir. They frequented Kabul throughout the year. The second type was Pakistani visitors who came to Kabul in the summer to escape the soaring temperatures. They usually stayed to witness the celebrations of Afghan Independence Day for a whole week. When the *khadem* saw this visitor he assumed that he must be Pakistani. There were few Pakistanis in Andrabi especially in autumn. If they came at all he knew about their summer habits of staying in rows of dirty, old apartments, located two kilometers away from the centre of the city.

Neither the *khadem* nor the visitor initiated a conversation with each other. At noon prayer time Rabani took his place in the mosque to lead the *namaz*. When the *namaz* was over the stranger approached Rabani and spoke to him in Arabic. It was only then that the *khadem* realized that the visitor must be of Arab descent. Although the *khadem* did not understand a word of the stranger's conversation, he later discovered that he would be staying overnight. What he did not know at the time was that the stranger would not be staying only for one night, but five nights. After this, the mysterious visitor disappeared without leaving a trace of ever having set foot in Andrabi.

Three days after the departure of the stranger, Rabani was in his room holding up a letter and showing it to a group of his students. Rahmat was among them.

"We are blessed by Almighty Allah," Rabani said.

"Allah-o Akbar," One of the young men praised Allah.

"These days angels circled our sky to deliver a message. A message of Almighty Allah."

"God is great."

"We are now recognised by our brothers in Egypt. This letter confirms it."

"Praise Allah."

"They are our brothers and fight the infidels in their own country. They are called *Ikhwan al Muslimin* Muslim Brotherhood. I have been writing to them for many years and only now received a reply. Finally one of them came here to say that they would help us in our cause."

"What was the reason that they delayed it for so long?"

"Brother, they cannot not trust anyone anymore. The letter could easily have been written by the Egyptian police. Now that we are recognised, they also have given us a task."

"Allah is with us. Mullah Sahib, you guide us and we will do whatever is the will of Allah."

"Brothers, I will soon tell you what to do. The time has come for us to take action and make the people aware of our existence, *inshalah*."

A month later, after school exams and towards the end of the academic year, two men purposely carrying bottles in each hand, approached three school girls from the other side of a bridge. This bridge was frequently referred to as *pole larzanak*, the shaky bridge, a wooden suspension bridge. One of the men was Rahmat. As the girls passed the men, a liquid was thrown directly into the faces of the girls, who had no premonition of what was coming. They screamed violently as the liquid hit them, covering their faces and collapsing on the ground in agony.

They rubbed their faces and tore their clothes off desperately trying to remove the liquid. Passing pedestrians were shocked, but before anyone could react the two young men simply disappeared into the crowd. After their getaway, once assured that they were not being followed, Rahmat's companion asked him "Did you get a good aim? Did you get the acid in their faces? I think I got two of them!"

"Oh yes, I did. Sure, all of it, right in their faces," Rahmat confidently replied.

"Good – they will never appear with those short skirts at schools again!" The younger man said triumphantly.

Rahmat had lied. He was not convinced of the need for such an operation. He had a kind heart and his philosophy was that both Islam and modern education could go hand in hand. Of course, he could not admit that to this follower that he had not thrown the acid on the girls. He could not bring himself to. Fortunately, they had thrown away the bottles during their flight and there remained no proof to detect his lie. Rahmat had come on that very bridge to show his support for Rabani and carry out his orders. But when he was there he did not have the heart to throw acid on a girl's face, as he thought she was innocent. For him, it was the government that should be blamed not the girls. It was the government that encouraged girls to wear those kinds of clothes.

The mission had put Rahmat in a very difficult position. He loved Rabani for his Islamic knowledge, but he did not admire him for his active drive to convert Afghanistan into a fundamentalist Islamic society. He now dearly wished that he had not agreed to be part of the acid throwing team. But there was no going back. This was a matter of trust among Muslim brothers who were followers of Rabani. Besides, there was a strong bond between Rabani and Rahmat. Rahmat was Rabani's favourite student and had the biggest potential to guide Muslims like him in the future. Rahmat knew all these things and yet he could not disagree to such action. He wanted to remain Rabani's favourite.

The following day newspapers and radio stations across Afghanistan broadcasted the acid-throwing story. When no one took responsibility for the dreadful act people guessed that it must be the work of Muslim fundamentalists. One thing was clear after the acid throwing incident: many people of Kabul and other cities began disliking the fundamentalists. This was a minor setback for Mullah Rabani. He took a lower profile, by not publically criticising the government for a while, and never mentioned women again in his formal *khotba,* lecture on Friday prayers.

Two weeks after the acid-throwing incident, at precisely twenty-five minutes past midnight, there was a knock on Rahmat's family door. Two men dressed in police uniforms asked for Hamid. Rahmat was taken aback and was going to confess the truth about the horrible acid-throwing incident that had been the source of his nightmares. He was ready to admit his part and clear his brother of it, but the officers did not even look at him. Instead, they searched the house and went through the two young men's books and papers, obviously searching for documents. They did not find what they were looking for. One of them finally lost his patience and slapped Hamid hard in the face.

"Where is it, you communist?' he asked. Hamid rubbed his cheek with the palm of his hand to lessen the painful impact of the slap. When he did not answer fast enough, the policeman slapped him on the head and asked him again.

"Where is it?" Hamid's mother was horrified and shouted. "Don't hit him you merciless fool. What are you looking for? What are you accusing him of?"

"Don't say anything you old woman and keep out of this! Your son is spreading *shabnama* night letters, criticising the government and has hidden them somewhere. This rat is operating at night like many other cowards like him."

They could not find anything in the house to show that Hamid was spreading *shabnama,* but the police did not give up. They forced Hamid into a police car. The night swallowed the wailing of a mother, seeing her son being carried away by the cruel police.

"These rats are becoming bolder," One of the policemen said.

"Yes, some days ago they threw acid on the face of school girls and now they are spreading *shabnama,* the son of bitches."

"You don't know the difference."

"What?"

"They are not the same group. The ones who threw the acid are Muslim fanatics and these rats are communists. These *haramis,* bastards are more dangerous to us. Fanatics hate women and they hate us. But these *haramis* want Russians to come and fuck their mothers. They want to give our country to Russians in the name of communism"

"But why do they spread *shabnama*?"

"Because they are cowards and because we will not allow these rats to publish their poisoning words in our newspapers. They are idiots. We watch them closely and they think that they can do whatever they want during the night. They are no better than thieves. They strike at night."

Hamid was pushed into a dark room in the police station. The room was locked and he was left alone in the darkness. Police were too tired or too upset to deal further with Hamid. It was a very dark, damp and cold room. There was a small window with steel rods, which blocked out any thoughts of escaping, allowing the moonlight to penetrate in the room from above. Only the moonlight permitted Hamid to see the shadowy outlines of the room, which consisted of four solid bare walls. There was no chair to sit on, no bed to lie on, but a long table positioned close to the edge of the wall. The room had a distinct foul smell of urine and blood.

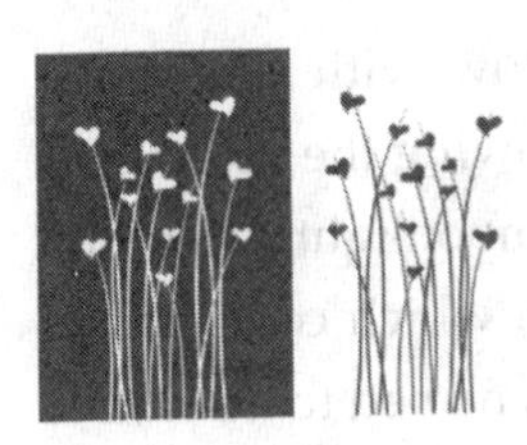

CHAPTER 11

The following day, Hamid's father came to the police station enquiring about his son. The family could not sleep that night. Hamid's mother was crying the whole night and his father was worried. Worrying was the only thing that he could do. It was a well known fact that when a person was in police custody, it was difficult to get him out, especially if the person did not have any connection with government officials or important people. The only way to get someone out was to bribe the police officers or bring someone important whom the police feared themselves, like a high-ranking officer working for the government. Abdul, Hamid's father had none. While he was waiting outside the police station, no one came to ask him the reason that he was there. It took him quite a while to find the courage to enter the office of the senior police officer. He greeted the officer but was ignored.

On the sofas on two sides of the room, opposite the walls there were five men; two senior police officers and three civilians were chatting, laughing, drinking tea, and smoking, but not paying any attention to Abdul who was standing by the door. Sometimes, the men looked at the poor man and each time he opened his mouth to say something, they started their own conversation, as if it was some kind of a game, prolonging the suffering of Abdul. Finally, the man who was seated behind a big desk rang a bell on top of his desk. Immediately, a junior police officer entered the room and after a formal greeting, which was a custom, said, "Yes Sir!"

"Why do you let these people enter my room, when I have an important meeting with my friends?" he asked, glancing at Abdul.

"Sir, I tried my best but he was not listening. Sorry Sir; he is an old man."

"Listen, this is the last time that you allow people enter my room without my permission, you understand?"

"Yes Sir," the junior police officer replied and took Abdul's arm to lead him out. But Abdul struggled to keep himself in and pleaded, "Sir, please let me explain." The man behind the big desk become impatient and raised his voice, shouting, "What do you want to explain old man?"

Before Abdul could say anything he asked the junior police officer "what is the issue?"

"Sir, he is the father of the boy that we brought here last night. The boy is anti-government."

"No, no Sir, he is not anti-government. My son is law abiding. He never had any trouble with law or anyone else. You can check your files Sir," Abdul pleaded.

"Listen to me old man! Don't tell me who is innocent and who is not. We know who is innocent. Now you go home and don't waste my time, unless you want to be locked up as well."

Abdul wanted to talk more, to make the police officer understand, to attract his sympathy; but he was pushed out of the office by the junior police officer. Tears trickled down Abdul's cheeks. He left the police compound broken-hearted. He wondered how to give the news to his wife, how to make her calm. Their son that they raised with love was in the custody of cruel men.

Hamid and his comrades were naive to think that the government was not aware of their activities. The government had its spies everywhere and they were well informed about activities of the left wing groups or so-called Afghan communists. The government feared them because they were well organised and they had foreign support. While the government ignored the Muslim Brotherhood, it vigilantly kept an eye on the activities of leftist groups. There was a good reason for that. The Muslim Brotherhood at that moment were trying to correct the population by taking actions such as forcing women to stay at home, but not so much involved, at least directly in activities harm the government. They were not popular and had a small number of followers.

Abdul's wife and their son Rahmat were waiting impatiently at home and as soon as he arrived she asked him, "What happened?"

"They say he was involved with some political activities against the government."

CHAPTER 12

Nobody knew that Golo and Safa were more than just neighbours. They had been seeing each other for a while. Golo kept his relationship hidden from his best friend Hamid and Safa did the same, not informing Roshan what was going on between her and Golo. It was all to do with protecting the honour of Safa. Golo and Safa became close when he began sending her elegantly composed love letters. He had not written them himself. He knew how intelligent Safa was and was too afraid to even attempt to write a love letter without making mistakes, never mind adding the kind of poetic prose that could charm a young woman's soul. There was however, Hamid, the poet who was excellent in writing love letters. God only knows how many love letters Golo gave in secret to Safa and how many times he begged his friend to write another one, until finally Safa agreed to accept Golo's love. Her condition was that nothing would develop between them until they got married.

This was a great triumph for Golo and at the beginning he was satisfied with the exchange of love letters between him and Safa. To have someone to love in this way for Safa was perfectly acceptable as long as she did not cross the line of meeting him. Golo was very handsome and the son of a rich man who had almost everything he wanted. Safa was very happy the way things were, but soon Golo was not satisfied anymore with just the letters. He was ready to move on to the next step of being the lover, to see her in the parks and in other hidden places where Kabulis met their sweethearts. There was a desire in him to talk to her and tell her how much he loved her and how much he wanted to be with her. Those letters were not his own words; they were written by his friend.

He spent many nights gazing at stars from his window, knowing that Safa was sleeping just across the courtyard. Sometimes he went behind the window of the room, shut his eyes and held his breath to hear Safa breathing during her sleep. He had thought that when Safa accepted his love, life would become easier for him. But he was wrong.

Now that Safa was responding, he wanted more. Finally, Safa agreed to meet him because she realized that Golo was in pain.

Safa and Golo met in a park and sat under a tree, away from the curious eyes of others, enjoying each other's physical presence for the first time. No one came their way and slowly they gained confidence, became comfortable with their surroundings and began talking passionately. Every now and then they gazed deep into each other's eyes with undivided attention, oblivious to their surroundings and the beauty of the scenery. Safa wore a midi laced dress of stretch fitted fabric, which she had bought a year ago from a fashionable store in Shahr-e Naw. It was a half sleeve dress which displayed her shapely smooth arms. To cover them modestly she wore a thin woollen black shawl on her shoulders; nevertheless the stretched figure hugging dress clearly showed off her attractive body curves.

"Believe me, I am so happy to finally see you alone," Golo greeted her with a smile.

"Me too," replied Safa shyly.

"No that can't be true. Otherwise you would have agreed to meet me a long time ago," Golo complained.

"Golo jan, this is very difficult for a woman," insisted Safa.

"If I share something, will you believe me?" asked Golo

"Tell me," Safa reassured him.

"I spent many a nights sitting outside your window."

"What?" Safa giggled in disbelief.

"Don't laugh, it is true," Golo said nervously.

"What were you doing there?" Safa asked.

"If I tell you more, you would only laugh more at me."

"No, do tell me and I won't laugh," Safa said, trying to control her laughter when she realized that Golo was serious.

"So many nights I have spent outside your window, straining to hear you breathing," Golo confessed while he held Safa's left hand.

"Don't joke," Safa said. She could not help laughing.

"I swear on the Koran," he declared.

"I don't believe you. Roshan says that you love sleep and even the sound of a bomb blast could not wake you. Don't think I don't know you," Safa said and laughed.

"What does Roshan know about love? What does she know about my feelings for you? Only a lover can know what I feel for you. Please don't be cruel to me. Agree to meet me at least once a week. I cannot eat and sleep without seeing you. I am deeply in love," Golo said, pleading with his eyes.

"Golo jan, I came once because of your pleas, but can't repeat this again," Safa explained.

"Safa jan, for Allah's sake just once a week," Golo begged.

"Oho, I am explaining why I can't see you anymore and yet you demand that I must meet you once a week. My father and mother will kill me if they find out. And, it is not only my father and mother. What about the society and my studies?"

"I am also studying; we both have final exams looming," Golo argued in desperation,

"Have you not heard of the acid throwing incident?" Safa tried to reason with Golo, "These people are vicious. I am scared."

"Of course, I know of what happened on the shaky bridge, pol-e larzanak," he admitted.

"I use the very same path and cross that bridge daily. Those girls were after all from my school," Safa elaborated on the reality of the risk.

"Safa, be sure that no one can harm you," Golo affirmed.

"How can you be so sure?" Safa queried.

"I can take you to school every day if you allow," he said protectively.

"Don't be ridiculous! I can't be seen with you."

"Let them throw acid on me."

"Ha, ha, ha, my hero. What a horrible thing to say. Why did those innocent girls get hit? Their only crime was going to school. What kind of person could do that? When I heard about it I could not sleep that night. What if they do it again?"

"The world is full of crazy people and that is the reason why I am asking you not to refuse meeting me. Life is unpredictable."

"Golo, you always use some incident for your benefit. I told you that I can't meet you. Imagine if the people who can't tolerate girls going to school caught us in public? If my parents find out that I am going out with you the least they could do is to stop me from going to school. They might think that I have used my school time to date be with you. They will think that I am capable of lying and that would be too bad for my reputation."

At that moment no one could have known the future of this couple, blinded by the rays of youthful and innocent love. Only eight days after their first meeting, Safa found herself sitting in Golo's car heading towards a beautiful valley twenty kilometers north of Kabul called Charikar, famous for its vineyards, big walnut trees, hillsides full of wild flowers, rivers running along the valleys. She knew about the beauty of this place from her father who once told her that the fragrance of the sinjid tree in a full moon light brought romance in his heart; and he missed his wife while he was away from home. Golo had sent a letter inviting her on a scenic drive. Safa thought about it and initially wanted to reject the idea, but finally couldn't resist. She had never travelled in a private car through a scenic valley; and she was convinced that she too was deeply in love with Golo and wanted to be with him. She wanted to see what her father had seen many years ago.

It was a sunny spring day and the earth smelled of freshness. The mountains of the Kabul valley were covered with an abundance of wild flowers and tulips. In school she had read many poems about the beauty of spring, but had never paid attention to real natural beauty before. Sitting next to Golo in the passenger seat, she viewed their surroundings through the eyes of her beloved. Small stalls on the roadside offered doogh, a drink made with sour yogurt, peppermint, cucumber, salt and water. The ingredients were simple and yet delicious. Golo stopped the car and bought two glasses of doogh.

"You know, it is the water content that makes doogh so delicious," Safa said, sipping her drink at the roadside stop.

"No, no. I think it is the fresh yoghurt that these rural people produce. We don't have this kind of good quality in Kabul city. By the time the yoghurt reaches Kabul, it is no longer fresh," Golo said, convinced of this theory.

"I bet you it is the amazing water! It has the freshness of spring water which these people collect from the mountains. The clear snow water, cool and inviting; full of minerals," Safa asserted, trying to prove her point.

"Well, there is no lab to prove which one of us is right," Golo continued, laughing.

At that very moment a village boy appeared with a bouquet of wild flowers. Golo gallantly bought them and offered them to Safa, saying "flowers for my flower."

This won a satisfied smile from her. It was a perfect day that God had dedicated to love.

He steered the wheel with one hand and held Safa's hand in the other. Half way to their destination they stopped at Istalif, a village famous for its wonderful clay pots ranging from dark brown, brown, red, black, green to deep blue.

There was no urgency in travelling and Golo drove leisurely. He wanted to revel in the beauty of the valley of Istalef.

"Takht-e Istalef was built by Babur," Safa said.

"Oh, Babur?"

"Yes, you mentioned his name in your letter."

"Yes, this king is my favourite poet."

"He called this place his takht, his throne, because in the summer he came here and received people."

They visited one of the village factories and ordered an *Istalifi Sofali* clay pot in blue and green with a motif of flowers. They requested that their names to be added on it as well and were told that their order would be ready the following week. They both knew that it was a perfect excuse to repeat this outing.

در کارگه کوزه گری رفتم دوش
دیدم دو هزار کوزه گویا و خموش
ناگاه یکی کوزه بر آورد خروش
کو کوزه گر و کوزه خر و کوزه فروش

Safa recited this poem and said: "It is a poem by Khayam. Please let me explain the philosophy behind it. The poet says: I went to pottery workshop and I saw two thousand clay pots, some quiet and some talking. Suddenly, one of them shouted: Where are those who made clay pots, those who bought them and those who sold them? The poem says enjoy the moment before you become a clay pot yourself one day.

Safa's barriers were now broken. She desired to be with Golo just as much as he wanted to be with her. She did not worry about her studies anymore. In fact, Safa was convinced that she could concentrate much better now that she had fallen in love.

Finally, they reached their destination. They entered a private garden owned by one of Golo's friends; a garden full of vineyards, fruit trees and a creek running along its boundary. They spent the rest of the day there, talking and laughing.

They were truly in love and getting deeper into it.

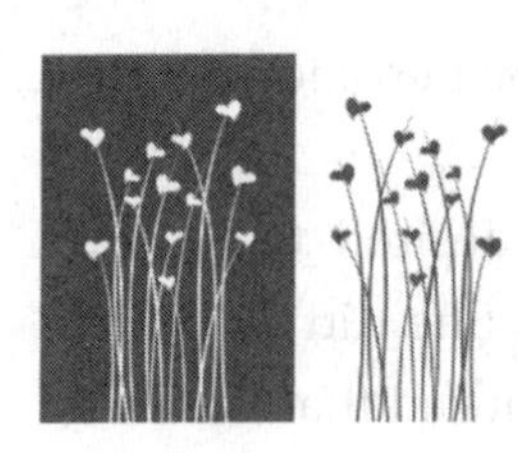

CHAPTER 13

Golo loved movies. Not a single week passed without him watching at least one film. Films and its actors had a great impact on him. Sometimes life felt like a scene from one of the movies and he an actor therein. His favourite actor was Clint Eastwood. He sometimes spent hours in front of the mirror to mimic Clint. He had occasionally received comments that he looked like Clint Eastwood and was even nicknamed Clint. After watching *A Fistful of Dollars,* he appeared with a hat and poncho. That was too much and he was ridiculed by his friends. He dropped the poncho and the hat, but not Clint as his nickname. God only knows how he found the money to shop at the most expensive store, Hamidi in Shahr-e Naw. He was one of their best regular clients. Girls loved his rough look and he was aware of their admiring secret glances. He was ridiculously handsome.

Safa was head over heels in love. She wanted to be with Golo as often as possible. The only problem was finding the time and she did not dare sacrifice school time to go out with Golo. So she started to lie and make excuses like going to the house of a friend to study or saying that she was going shopping after school. Her family trusted her, so no one doubted her. A week later she was sitting in Golo's car again, heading to the north.

The road was lined with fine, tall trees, their trunks painted white up to a metre's height. The whiteness of the trunks contrasted with the green foliage and created an image of a long tunnel, with a green ceiling and white chalk sidewalls. Golo drove with windows open. The wind blew through Safa's hair. She tried to manage her hair, constantly pushing it away from her face and yet loved the wind caressing it. Golo watched her from the corner of his eyes and noticed the smile on her face. The unconscious smile expressed satisfaction and playfulness of the moment. She wore a short-sleeved blue cotton blouse, a white pleated skirt, the fashion of the times, and short socks with tennis shoes. She was intensely observed by Golo from head to toe. Her smooth curves showed through her summer clothes and filled him with desire. Love was in her heart at that splendid hour that was filled with the beauty of nature. Nature had presented her the magic of love. She was filled with joyous love towards him, towards nature and towards herself. Safa saw the beauty of love in everything that she set her eyes upon.

Golo was driving confidently, mostly watching Safa, instead of the road. He cracked jokes to make her laugh, and joined in the popular songs on the radio:

Don't say no to a kiss
When the warmth of summer fills your heart
When the music of birds fills your soul
When the fragrance of flowers intoxicates you
O my love, don't say no.

Suddenly Golo heard Safa scream: "Watch out!"

Golo pressed his foot on the brake and Safa pushed her hands towards the window shield to avoid hitting it. Golo felt embarrassed and enquired gently if she was fine. She smiled back reassuringly. From behind the trees, they saw hundreds of cows, goats, sheep, mules and horses crossing the road, guided by a few men and women. They were *koochis,* nomads, who travelled from Pakistan to Afghanistan, in search of green pastures for their cattle. This was their life, back and forth. Winters were spent in the warmth of Pakistan and summers in

the attractive milder and cooler climate of Afghanistan. The crossing of the animals took a while. At the tail end, a tall woman carried a lamb on her shoulders, her shapely rounded breasts visible under her dark red dress. She wore no scarf to hide her hair; her pitch black hair shone brightly reflecting the sun. Safa had heard about these women from her father. They were renowned for their courage and love. Her father once related of an incident when he was walking behind a *koochi.* She was obviously pregnant and suddenly left the crowd to squat behind a rock. Safa's father assumed that it was nature's call, but just a few minutes later she came back with a newborn child! These women were also known to express themselves in certain type of poems referred to as *landay*. They never wrote them down because they were illiterate. However, their stories and emotions were born through recitals. Those who heard them passed them to one another and occasionally a line was recorded by a literate audience. Safa recalled reading one of these poems in a book or a magazine sometime ago and remembered how erotic some of the emotions had been:
Dear god, convert me into a shirt
For my lover to wear me day and night

The countryside smelt of sinjid trees in full blossom, mingled with the nostalgic smell of wheat, wild flowers and earth. A wasp entered the car and Safa started waving her arms up and down to shoo the wasp away, more panicked than confident in her gestures. With these movements her skirt rose up her leg. Golo drove with one hand tried to assist Safa to get rid of the wasp. In reality he was mesmerised by the erotic sight of her naked thighs, smooth like the purest of white marble. The wasp was so stubborn that Golo had to pull up on the side of the road. They got out of the car laughing and let the wasp find its own way out before continuing their journey.

A few hours later they reached their destination – a huge garden with tall walls and big chenar trees planted along the walls to create privacy. Even the gardeners were nowhere to be found. Golo had arranged this to secure the privacy he craved with Safa. On the takht, a beautiful Persian carpet, lay by the wall shaded by an old chenar tree. *Takias,* long elongated pillows, were set along the wall. They took off their shoes, peered at the fruit trees lying down on the eloquent surrounds and listened to the symphony of summer. The world was music and birds were the orchestra. They lay side by side on the carpet with their backs resting on the *takias*. Safa's left hand lay near to Golo's. She shut her eyes, listened to the birds and inhaled the fragrance of wild flowers, dreaming. This place reminded her of Nijrab where she was born. She loved wild gardens like this in the countryside. In Nijrab, after a typically cooked lunch in a *tanoor,* a clay stove which produced the mixed smell of burning wood, fresh *tandoori* bread, vegetables and chicken – she lay under a big chenar tree and slept much of the afternoon away.

Her cousins collected mulberries from the trees and dropped them in a *kariz,* a spring. The sporting challenge was to pick twenty mulberries, dip your hands in the water twenty times, without them freezing. The water in the *kariz* originated from the ice capped mountains and was ice cold. Safa never managed to dip her hands in more than fifteen times.

Golo moved over to Safa's side and watched her closely. Her eyes were shut and she appeared to be dreaming. This encouraged him to move his hand slowly towards hers, not sure how she would react. Would she pull away? There was only one way to find out. He moved his hand towards hers very slowly, fearing that she would open her eyes any moment and question his act. Golo was not usually shy, but the power of love was intimidating. Anyone would have felt shy in the presence of Safa – a beautiful and extremely intelligent girl, brought up with eastern conservativeness. He knew that she was falling in love with him; otherwise she would not have risked coming out here with him alone. He decided to not touch her hand, but raised his body instead, resting on his stomach and gazing down to study Safa's face. Her skin was smooth, her cheeks had blushed a faint pink with no signs of make-up, her black eyebrows were thinly shaped and rested above her eyelids, her eyelashes were long and naturally curved and her lips were as poetic as red roses. His face was so near hers that he could feel his breath caressing her face and at that moment she suddenly opened her eyes.

Golo almost pulled away but she smiled at him. "I love you Safa, I love you so much," Golo said. She did not reply but kept smiling. He reached towards her neck and pushed her hair away with his hand. Encouraged by the lack of a negative reaction, he pulled himself closer and kissed her neck gently. The kiss sent electrical vibrations through Safa's body and she moved up in response, only to meet Golo's lips with her own, somewhat intuitively, without giving it a conscious thought. Golo assumed that she wanted to respond with a deeper and more intensive kiss. Safa started to pull away. She wanted to show Golo her love, but did not want close physical or sexual contact.

"Please stop Golo, I beg you."

"I can't Safa, I can't. I have been waiting for this moment since I met you."

"But you promised that we would not touch."

"I'm sorry Safa for breaking my promise. Believe me. Just a kiss, nothing more."

"No, no."

"I promise, just a kiss."

She was pinned to the ground and Golo was now on top of her. She could not resist him anymore and soon kissed him back intensely.

Her body was hot with desire and she felt Golo's erection against her. Such a response provoked Golo to go further and touch her thighs. This time Safa pushed him away with strength and jumped off the takht and threatened to leave if he did not stop immediately. Golo calmed down and finally settled for an innocent kiss from then on. They melted with each kiss. That was the extent of their heat and sweat in the magical moments spent in the beautiful garden. The bruises on their lips were evidence of their many and passionate kisses.

Romancing in the garden did not relieve Golo's sexual tension; it was becoming increasingly worse. He was constantly in a state of erection. His time alone in the garden with Safa triggered increasing restlessness and desire to seduce her and to enjoy their youth.

Finally, one day they made love in the same garden.

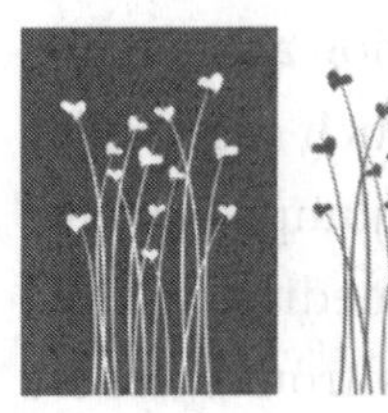

CHAPTER 14

"Roshan, I don't want one of your silly tricks again," Nasrin said.

Roshan had been caught filling dumplings with chilly again. It was her favourite joke. Whenever she helped cooking *mantu,* dumplings, she couldn't help but play this trick. The real laugh came later when the dish was served and some unlucky person got the piece filled with chilly. For her the joy of having this type of food was related more to the trick than in making it. During the meal she would wait for that moment when the person who bit on the chilly jumped, hit the roof and asked for water. Since, she played this game again and again, everyone knew who did it. Yet Roshan couldn't control herself when she was preparing the dumplings.

The women were busy making *mantu* and *ashak* dumplings at Nasrin's. Safa and Roya were there too. They enjoyed the day best while cooking delicious food and talking with each other. These friends got together to cook at least twice a month for meals. But for meals such as *samanak,* the food which was cooked on the first day of spring, at least fifty women met, shooed the men out for the night, and spent the entire night cooking and singing:

Samanak dar josh maa kapcha zanaim
Deegaran dar khaab maa boosa zanaim.
Samanak is boiling in the pot and we still stir it
Others are sleeping and I kiss my lover

Of course that was just a naughty song or wishful thinking of Afghan women. There were no men to kiss, since cooking *samanak* was a woman's only affair.

"Ah. Caught you again," Nasrin said, pretending to be angry.

"Are you the police, mother?" Roshan asked.

"And are you still baby, Roshan?" Nasrin snapped with real anger this time.

"Let her enjoy making it, Nasrin," Roya intervened.

"Roya jan, her time for these kinds of jokes has passed. I was married and already had two children when I was her age."

"Nasrin jan, my sister, that time is no longer. Girls didn't go to school those days. Now they do."

"Do they learn to fill dumplings with chilly at school?"

They all laughed. The smell of coriander, *gandana,* another vegetable, minced meat and other spices, ready to be cooked filled the women's nostrils. Roshan loved this smell since it was a special time to be with her friend Safa and her mother. The dish required many hands. The first woman was in charge of making the dough, spreading it on a wooden table, using a wooden roller to make it very thin and cutting it into pieces of 4 to 5 centimetre diameter. The second woman was responsible to prepare the half cooked minced meat, adding spices such as turmeric, coriander, chilli powder, garlic and onion. The third woman cut the *gandana,* a vegetable only used by Afghans. The first part consisted in cutting and cooking. Then the pieces of dough were filled with minced meat and *gandana*. The last stage was arranging the dumplings carefully on the first layer of a big steam pot that had holes in it. The bottom of the pot was filled with water to steam the dumplings.

The kitchen was filled with noise of laughter, jokes, gossip or simple stories of Nasrin and Roya's childhoods. In the background, music came from the living room. Recently Toftofi had bought a tape recorder and Roshan had taped Indian movie songs that were popular among the teenagers. Safa was in charge of making fresh lemon juice. It was a hot day and everyone drank some. As soon as a jug was empty another one was filled with fresh juice. After four hours of hard but enjoyable work, the food was ready. A *desterkhaan,* big white cloth, was laid at the centre of the living room and all the women sat around it cross-legged. Roshan sat next to Safa. She informed Safa that she had managed to place four chillies in the dumplings. They ate quietly as was the custom of the Afghans, that the mouth could be used either for eating or talking; and now that there was such good food in front of them, only idiots would want to talk. Suddenly one of them jumped off the *desterkhaan.* It was no other than Roshan. All three women laughed when she cried, sticking out her tongue and poured glass after glass of water down her throat. They said in chorus: *"chah kan da chaast"*. The person who digs the well will stay stuck in it. Safa wondered what happened to the three other dumplings. She did not realize yet that one of them would go to her father that evening and the two others will be passed on to a neighbour. It was a custom to share food with their neighbours. At least Golo would be safe.

After dinner *baghlawa,* a sweet pastry made with honey, was served with green tea. Toftofi had bought this desert some days ago on Nasrin's request. He knew exactly where to find the best *baghlawa* in Kabul.

Late afternoon Safa and Nasrin left. Roshan helped her mother tidy the house.

"You have to become more serious in life," Nasrin said.

"Oh, mother. I'm sorry. I thought you had forgotten the issue."

"That woman has been here many times."

"What woman?"

"The one that you met in the *hamam.*"

"Which woman?" Roshan had forgotten all about the incident at the hamam.

"You know which woman, Roshan. She helped you there."

"Oh khodaa that? You mean that woman who claimed to be my aunt?"

"She has a son in Germany."

"What do you want me to do about it?"

"She has asked for you to marry her son."

"No, mother. Please don't joke."

"I'm serious. Time has come for you Roshan."

"Mother jan, please. I even don't like that woman."

"Listen Roshan, you don't need to like her. You will be married to her son and will be away. You will be in Germany."

"Mother, please don't send me away so far. What about my education?"

"Roshan, don't bring education as an excuse. You haven't been the top student and living in Germany will bring you security and happiness. Why do you want to stay in this country anyway?"

"But mother..."

"There is no but about it. Your father and I have been thinking about it for the past two months. We did not say yes to her yet. But now that we've checked everything, we're satisfied."

"So you have already decided and I have not even finished school yet?"

"We will let you finish school to prove that we are not bad parents. We will show you the photo of your future husband. We also agreed that he could call you on the phone from time to time. I'm sure that you will find the arrangement good for you."

That night Roshan cried for a long time. She was sad that to have finished her favourite food and was scared about her uncertain future. She wondered if pleasure was always associated with pain.

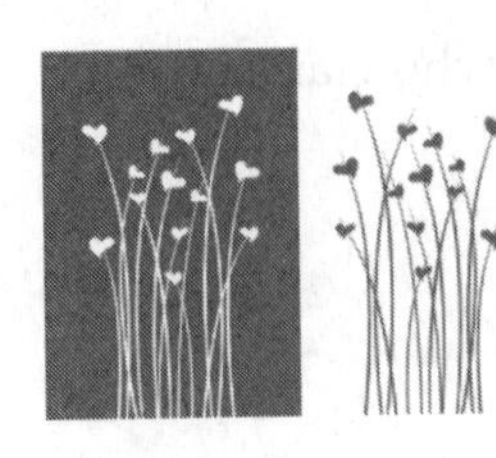

CHAPTER 15

The time came for Kabul University entrance results to be publicly announced. Safa was among the students that scored top marks and was accepted into the faculty of medicine. Roshan was less fortunate, but nevertheless managed to be accepted into the teaching institute. This field did not require special qualifications in Afghanistan. The outcome did not bother her very much. In two months time she was destined to be married and would leave Kabul for good. It was a half arranged marriage. The son of a distant relative of Roshan's father, living in Germany, was now eligible for marriage and decided to return to his home country to marry a proper girl from Kabul. The boy was somewhat conservative, despite having lived in Germany since he was 15. He was still influenced by the eastern way of life and openly wished to find a wife with the same values. His father was delighted with the news and felt that having a daughter-in-law brought up in Kabul customs would make life easier for the entire family.

The father sent a message to Roshan's family. He recalled that Totofi had a daughter about the same age as his son. Roshan's father was equally delighted with the prospect of such a marriage and wasted no time, allowing Roshan to spend time talking on the phone and exchanging photos with her future husband. Telephone dating was one of the few courtships permitted in their culture. They liked each other's facial features and had sufficient things in common to get along as they got acquainted over the phone. For Roshan it seemed like a good opportunity and better than marrying someone in Kabul.

She had heard many times how developed, modern and beautiful Germany was.

Golo was the least fortunate of all in the university entrance results. He was not accepted in any faculty or institution. Deep inside he knew it would have been an uphill battle to enter university. For someone who could not even write a letter this was surely not a realistic dream. He shrugged to prove that he did not care and had everything that he could wish for already. The traditional idea was that university was the only way to obtain the required qualifications to secure a job and to settle down with a family.

This did not apply in his case. He did not need qualifications, given that he already had a family job, and the truth was that his father had asked him many times to help with work in the family merchant business. He already had the prospect of starting his own family, at least that was the way he saw it. He was going to be the husband of one of the most beautiful and intelligent girls of Kabul, who would be the mother of his children. He loved Safa and was equally convinced that Safa loved him in return. Golo was sure of his choice. She had made the decision to be his wife on the day that they were in that beautiful garden in the north and she had allowed her virginity to be taken away – a day that had occurred long before the university entrance results were announced.

A few days after the university results came out, Safa was in Golo's room. They were addicted to each other and Golo's room had become their love nest. It was much more convenient than being outside since no one could see them together. It was way past midnight and everybody was fast asleep. The door was shut, making sure no one entered unannounced. Golo was careful yet sure that his parents would never bother checking on him. He always had complete privacy. At night he turned the dim light on his bed table. Safa could see the walls of his room decorated with posters of Iranian and Indian film stars and three big posters of Bruce Lee. A keen sportsman, he went to a karate club almost every afternoon and had seen all of Bruce Lee's films, when they were screened at the cinema. There were shelves full of sport magazines and music cassettes. Every night before he went to bed he listened to music and looked at a sports magazine. Tonight he was listening to *Shehnai*. The volume of the cassette player was so low that it was impossible to be heard beyond the closed door. Safa was sitting next to him on the bed with her back supported by the wall. Her eyes were closed, listening to the music with her heart. Golo's left hand was on her shoulder, sometimes caressing her long hair.

"So next year you will be going to university?" Golo asked.

"Yes, God willing."

"For me it is the end of the road. I was tired of school anyway. I'm glad it is over."

"I'm really sorry Golo. I wish I could help."

Without saying a word, Golo got up, moved to one of the cupboards and brought a packet of cigarettes that he had been hiding. He put a cigarette to his lip and offered one to Safa.

"Would you like to have a puff?"

"No, I don't want."

"I only smoke when I am celebrating."

Safa was puzzled. "Celebrating what?"

"I am celebrating your success and mine. Your's to continue studying and mine to finally get rid of all these books and papers. Thank you Allah! You are kind."

For Safa, blinded by love and yet dedicated to her studies, such comments did not shock her.

CHAPTER 16

There is no difference between funerals and weddings for Kabuli families blessed with daughters: they cry bitterly on both occasions. When a girl gets married, the parents cry knowing their daughter's future visits will not be frequent and that it is likely that she will not keep in regular touch with her previous friends. Her life changes because after marriage she belongs to a new household and her husband becomes her master. For Roshan it was twice as difficult. She was not only going to a new household, but also to a foreign country with a different language, different customs and different climate. She knew that it would be a different life altogether.

Safa was no less sorry of her friend's departure. She had not only been her best friend, but was now her future sister-in-law. She knew in all likelihood that she would not see Roshan again for many years, if at all. When girls married boys living abroad, coming home for a visit was a dream that did not necessarily come true. For this reason both young women cried hard at the wedding party. Two days later Roshan boarded a plane to Germany to her new home with her newly wedded husband by her side. She did not cry anymore, thinking instead of how lucky she was to have an educated husband living in Europe.

In the loneliness following Roshan's departure, Safa was even more drawn to Golo. She now met him regularly in his room. They made love as often as they could find space and time. One day the inevitable consequence of naive young fools blinded by love and lust brought unwanted news to them.

Safa lay next to Golo and said, "I think I am pregnant, Golo." Golo jumped in shocked anguish.

"No, no! How do you know?" Golo asked.

"I missed my period three weeks ago. It has never happened to me before," Safa replied with anxiety in her voice. Golo was speechless, searching for the right words.

"I thought that we had been careful?" That was the only thing he could think of.

"I suppose we were not careful enough. Oh my God, what will my parents say! They will surely kill me. My father is so happy that I entered university and now, his dream and mine are shattered," Safa said sobbing. "These kinds of events make me want to disappear off the face of the earth."

"My love, please don't be upset and don't worry. I will marry you as soon as you want. I love you and having a child is not a problem for me," Golo comforted her. "In fact, let's get married as soon as possible. I love you Safa and I want to be the father of our child," Golo continued emotionally.

"Golo, you are forgetting an important detail. For my father and me education is more important than anything else. I love you too, but it is not yet time for marriage and children. Of course, I want to get married to you and have your children but only when I finish university. Golo, I want to be a doctor."

That night, Safa cried her heart out no matter how much Golo tried to console her. She was miserable. They both lost the desire to make love for the first time since they began dating.

The lovers were not prepared for this. They had only thought about love and happiness and now real life was presenting them a great challenge. They were not the only fools in love who woke up one day from their dream and faced a nightmare. That was the reason that boys and girls were kept separated until marriage. If a mistake happened and a girl got pregnant there was only one solution: marriage.

At 9 o'clock one morning, two months after Safa had missed her period, Golo and Safa walked the narrow streets of Barana, an old part of Kabul. A local healer resided here, famous for performing society's forbidden tasks such as abortions. Golo had discovered the woman healer with great difficulty. He did not wish to reveal the identity of the person needing the abortion and that made it increasingly difficult to inquire about the healer's whereabouts. Two days before Golo had gone there alone to make sure he knew how to find the healer's house and to ensure that she was available to do the task. On his search he had to ask directions several times and was relieved that Safa had not accompanied him. People would surely have guessed the reason Golo was accompanying Safa and why they were searching for this particular address.

Fortunately, the woman agreed to perform the abortion but against a huge sum of money. Golo was trapped and had no other choice. Healers always requested large fees to perform abortions. There weren't many naughty Kabuli girls who got pregnant. The healer did not have many customers and the few ones she had, were ashamed enough to pay good money for their sins. After all she was not in a business that could be considered decent. This type of occupation was considered to be immoral and had its price. Golo stole and sold one of his mother's jewels to pay for the abortion.

Safa was scared. She shivered at the thought of the horrid stories she'd heard of girls experiencing genital damage or abundant loss of blood after an abortion at the hand of a healer. Walking on the narrow street in view of the local residents had not been easy. She felt the gaze of each passersby and the intensity of their curious eyes, as if they knew the reason of her presence there. She felt guilty and ashamed and was cursing herself for her weakness to have allowed the situation to get out of control. They passed a small shop at the entrance of an archway. People sat on either side of the shop and the air carried the smell of hashish. The archway was dark and Safa felt that the alley was never ending.

As they passed through the archway, the foul smell of open sewage shocked Safa's nostrils and she reached for her handkerchief. The street zigzagged and they passed under a smaller archway into an alley as dark as the night. Safa grabbed Golo's hand and started crying quietly. At the end of the second alley was a small door. Golo banged on it with his fist, but no one opened. It took him some time to adjust to the darkness and managed to find a piece of stone to knock on the door. Finally, after what seemed to be an eternity, the door opened and a female voice enquired who was there. Golo responded and they entered the house.

Beyond the doorway was a grim courtyard with dirty water standing on its surface. They went up a staircase and reached a small room. There was barely enough light to see the face of the healer. The woman looked at Safa and greeted her: "So this is the naughty girl!" She laughed and Safa noticed her yellow-brown teeth. Her hair was untidy, her face wrinkled and she wore clothes reeking of garlic. The woman turned to Golo and said, "You can come back in two hours." Golo left the house without a word. He didn't dare to say goodbye to Safa knowing that she was trembling with fear.

Two days later Safa woke up at the Kabul hospital. She had bled profusely during the abortion. The bleeding did not stop for another two days. Amazingly, she had managed to hide her deteriorating condition at home, but in the afternoon of the second day she collapsed from exhaustion and loss of blood. Her mother rushed her to the hospital. When she finally opened her eyes and found out where she was she wished that she had died instead. Facing such embarrassment would lead her to a life of being as good as dead. Her parents would never accept such shame and dishonour to her family. A young female doctor, appearing to be in her thirties, standing next to her, noticed that she was awake.

"How do you feel now?" she asked. Safa just managed to shake her head and tears immediately appeared at the corner of her eyes.

"I wish that I was dead instead of having to face my parents," she sobbed.

"You are young and should not say that," the doctor replied, trying to comfort her.

"But Doctor, my parents will never accept what I have done. They expected great achievements from me and never thought that I would end up like this."

"What you have done is wrong. Our society does not accept girls getting pregnant before marriage, but when you try to hide it and get rid of it, you make the problem even worse," the doctor said, as she injected her with some medicine. "Do you know how many girls lose their lives having abortions this way?"

"What difference does it make now, Doctor? I am or will be dead soon anyway. My parents will not let me live like this. I have brought big shame to the family."

"Nobody knows, nor needs to know what happened to you," the doctor assured her. "It is the policy of the hospital not to reveal the cause of such bleeding. The hospital is aware of the strong reaction of parents and relatives towards the girl who gets pregnant before marriage. After some unfortunate cases where girls in such circumstances lost their lives, the hospital decided to simply inform parents and relatives that the bleeding was due to an unfortunate situation," the doctor smiled understandingly. "I deliberately chose to talk to you without the presence of your mother. Now rest and don't worry too much. By the way the infection will cause you some pain and you will experience fever for at least two weeks. Moreover, I am not sure that you might ever be able to get pregnant again."

Safa missed university for two weeks and did not see Golo at all. The pain and fever were unbearable. When she finally managed to go back to university, she frequently thought about her life and what had happened to her. She was not even sure that she wanted to see Golo again for some time. Loss of concentration proved to be dangerous for her future medical studies. She had to get back to being a dedicated student above all else. However, she slowly realized that it had been too long since Golo had been to see her and began to worry. Although she was not keen to see him after the abortion, her desire to marry him had not changed. Anyway, who else would marry a girl who was no longer a virgin?

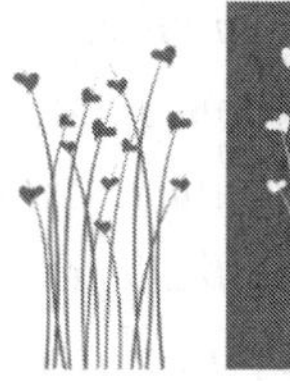 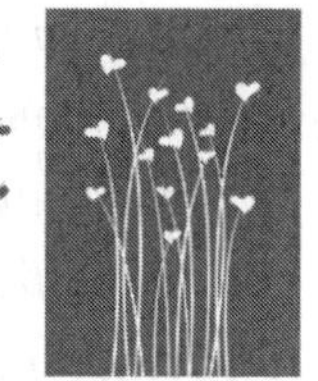

CHAPTER 17

Golo had disappeared.

He could not take the pressure any more. It had just been lust and when the problem appeared he lost interest in Safa. He considered himself lucky to have sexual experience with a beautiful and intelligent girl. Something that normally only exists in the minds of other young males of Kabul; who can only dream about such experiences. How could he fall in love, when his future was unclear he thought? Failing to enter university and not having a job was a problem. The glorified picture that he had painted to Safa about his father's import and export business was not realistic. He had been thinking of leaving Kabul for a long time. Young people like him often heard of men who immigrated to Iran and found jobs and personal enrichment. People talked about how well developed and progressive Iran was, almost like the West. He was also influenced by the Iranian movies that were screened in the cinemas of Kabul. One of his favourite daydream images was naked Iranian women surrounding him.

Golo was a spoiled child. His father could not prevent him from going to Iran. He had failed to prevent him from many things in life and his son's wish to leave was just another battle. After some philosophical reflection, the father decided to be happy for his son's decision. He thought that an Iranian experience might just convert the spoiled youth to manhood.

A month had passed before Safa discovered that Golo had left for Iran. A letter arrived in which Golo wrote:

My beautiful darling Safa, seeing you in such pain was unbearable for me. I felt your pain deep in my heart. Maybe I am to blame for having put you in this situation. In fact, I am ashamed that I was not strong enough to avoid physical contact. I'm sorry. I have left Kabul and am now in Iran. I'm living in a flat rented by a friend in Tehran and hoping to secure a job soon. Maybe it is right for the two of us to stay apart, at least until you have finished your studies and I have earned enough money to marry you. I love you and cannot wait for us to be together forever, united and married.

Golo could not stop himself from lying. As usual, the letter was written by someone else. It was the first and the last letter that Safa would receive from Golo in Iran.

Safa was devastated. In a short period of time her life had been turned upside down. First, with the news of her acceptance into the faculty of medicine, a dream she held on to throughout her teens. Her happiness, however, was short lived when she became pregnant. Then, in the bargain of the only solution she could foresee, she almost lost her life in the hands of a local healer. And if that was not enough, the man that she fell in love with, whom she had trusted with her body and soul had disappeared. Life should not have changed so much in a short period of time. Even Safa could not bear the pressure. She was known for her ability to accept many types of pressures in life, but nothing had prepared her for these series of shocks. The immediate impact was loss of appetite and concentration. She lost weight and worried constantly. Worries robbed her of sleep and this contributed to loss of concentration. She became convinced that she would fail her exams and be kicked out of the university. Her mother was the first to notice the change in Safa's appearance and behaviour, but assumed that it was the result of university pressure and facing new academic challenges. Safa was only too relieved to have her studies cover up and hide her real problems. She did not wish her mother to find out what really had happened to her hard working innocent daughter.

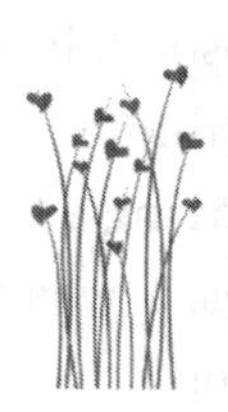 

CHAPTER 18

The sound of continuous rain on the window panes increased Safa's depression. The sky was grey and the courtyard was dark, giving a melancholy appearance to the trees and flowers. Raindrops flowed down the surrounding courtyard's mud walls, creating tiny streams, which carved their way to the bottom. Safa continued to gaze out of the window, unable to concentrate on reading or writing, the required daily academic commitment. Being in a top faculty demanded hard work every day. The rain produced a damp and humid smell in the room, mingled with the smell of mud that Safa did not like. Sunshine was required to change her mood, but for the past three days it had constantly rained. Spring in Kabul could be like this sometimes. It could rain for days. The season reminded her of that very spring when she had gone out with Golo. With Golo there had been no worries or sadness. Life had been momentarily joyous. She recalled her first kiss when they drove to the north. The first touch and the first promise. But promises were not meant to be broken. Now disillusioned, Safa wondered if people could lie about love, the most precious of all emotions, how could they be honest about other matters? She was angry with herself for having trusted Golo so easily. She cursed her weak heart for falling in love with a man who was not reliable.

Nasrin entered the room carrying a tea tray. Since Safa had enrolled in university, her mother had been more attentive. She knew that her daughter was studying hard in a highly competitive institution. Therefore, Safa was exempt from housework, unless she was absolutely needed and that only happened when they had visitors for dinner.

"Having a break?" Nasrin asked.

"Yes, I was watching the rain. This place becomes so dark when it rains."

"Is anything wrong?"

"No, I just don't like dark grim days."

"I hope this darkness is not due to difficulty with your studies."

Nasrin was very concerned. The family had given their entire support to their daughter's medical education. They believed that she would become a doctor one day. After all they had moved to the city, coming from a very modest background, with little choice. They could not compete with society because they were not wealthy. The only wealth they had was education. Since not all rich people made it to university, Safa's father, a university graduate, demanded that his daughter do even better than him.

"Oh mother, please don't worry," Safa replied. "I am fine with my studies. Just allow me some time to be the way I am. I promise that I will pass the university exams successfully."

"Safa jan, I was only concerned, but you know best. Now have your tea."

Nasrin poured the tea in a cup and left the room. Safa had lied. She was worried about her future on two fronts: she could not concentrate sufficiently on her studies, and her chance of ever finding a suitor in marriage, given she was no longer a virgin, seemed even more remote. She picked up her textbook, but realised that she had been stuck on the same page for ages. She dropped the book, took a notebook and started writing instead.

It has been a long time since we spoke. You are not by my side anymore and deep sorrow has penetrated my heart. You were my family. Of course, I have my mother and father, but I only shared my dreams, my happiness and my sadness with you. Where are you? How is life treating you? Do you remember me or has the foreign country erased me from your memory? If distance has helped you forget me, it has had a different impact on me. There isn't any day that passes when I don't think of you and miss you. It seems like you left only yesterday.

I never imagined that my life could change like this. My confidence is shattered and I am not the same girl who was once happy to be challenged by her teachers. Now I am afraid of them. In this country, women are born with sorrows and will die with sorrows. Maybe the time I spent with you was not real but just a dream. The dream has gone and has been replaced by reality, a nightmare.

I am sorry to bore you with my emotions. Let me tell you about our country instead. You probably want to know what is going on these days. The biggest news is the disappearance of the son of a general. There are many theories regarding this. Some say that men, hunting beautiful boys for their sexual pleasure, kidnapped him. Others say it was gangsters demanding money. Some even think it was a leftist group. That is the reason why police came to our class one day when one of my professors was lecturing and arrested him for the kidnapping of the boy. He was a leftist professor and a very bright person. I loved his lectures. Talking about the leftist group, I must say that they are becoming bolder in their activities. Recently they organised a demonstration at the city centre, stopping the flow of traffic. The police intervened and fighting broke out. There were a large number of demonstrators and they picked up some policemen and threw them into the river. Many policemen were injured and two were killed. They were conscripts from a poor background. It is ironic that the leftist group claims to protect poor people, but do not realise that the police are just peasants who migrated to the cities. Of course, I don't care about the officers. They are terribly corrupt and make too much illegal money.

She signed and tore the sheet of paper from her notebook. She placed the letter in an envelope and wrote Roshan's address.

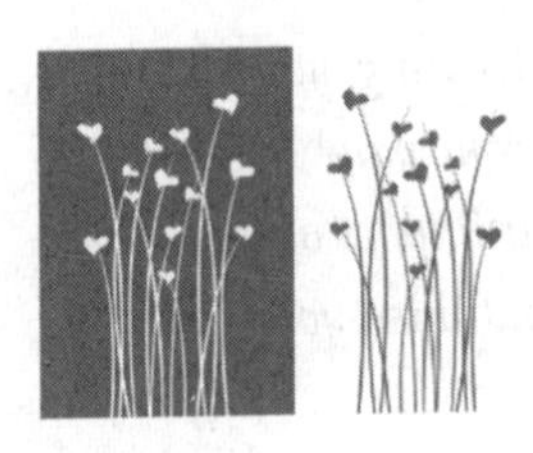

CHAPTER 19

At the end of the semester Safa was preparing herself to fail but a miracle happened. In reality, she caused the miracle to happen. Studying long hours after midnight compensated for her poor concentration. As she was conscious of her shortcoming she studied ten times harder. So the miracle was in fact earned. She just managed to pass the semester.

It was a university tradition for students to celebrate their success after months of hard work. Different faculties held concerts and performed plays to celebrate such milestones. Safa also felt that she deserved to celebrate after the many months of hard work and worries about her personal life. On the day she chose to attend the university auditorium a play was performed. She sat in the first row with her friends. The play started and she discovered that it was a comedy. Half way through the performance the entire auditorium was shaking with laughter. Safa laughed so hard that from time to time she held her stomach as tears rolled down her cheeks. She laughed and laughed and buried her sorrows under the screams and laughter. When the play was over, she jumped out of her seat and went backstage, requesting to meet with the playwright. A man appeared in front of her with puffed, tired eyes. It was Hamid.

Safa approached him and said, "I have never laughed so much in my life. Tears were pouring out of my eyes, and I was not the only one! All my friends felt the same. They could not control their wild laughter. Congratulations! I really don't know what to say, but thank you for making me laugh again after such a long time."

Hamid was delighted to hear a fan admiring his work. Usually, people who came backstage asked for actors, actresses or the director but rarely sought the playwright. "Well, I am glad that you liked it. I wish I could laugh as much as the audience did," Hamid responded graciously.

"I am sure that you laugh a lot in life. Otherwise you could not have written such a wonderful comedy, that caused such a storm in the auditorium," Safa continued.

"I wish I did! For me, behind that comedy and laughter, there is a deep message," Hamid explained.

"Oh I saw that. I know it is not a simple comedy. It is a critique of the social and political systems of our country," Safa said.

Hamid almost leapt with happiness at this revelation and exclaimed "That's it! That's it! I am glad that you understood the motive behind this comedy. The hidden message is much more important than the appreciation of comedy and laughter."

Safa smiled and said, "Don't worry; the message was not wasted on me. I love to read and see plays like this."

"Well as a matter of fact, I did not have any intention of seeing this play performed. I wrote an earlier version with a more direct critique of the political system in Afghanistan but the selection committee rejected it. I wrote this play in a very short period of time as a replacement for the first one."

"I would very much like to read that play sometime," Safa said eagerly.

"Do you really want to read it?" Hamid asked.

"Yes. I don't have any compelling studies right now. Exams have just finished and I can read just for pleasure," Safa replied.

"In that case, you are lucky because I have it with me. If you wait here, I will bring it to you," Hamid said and disappeared to fetch the manuscript.

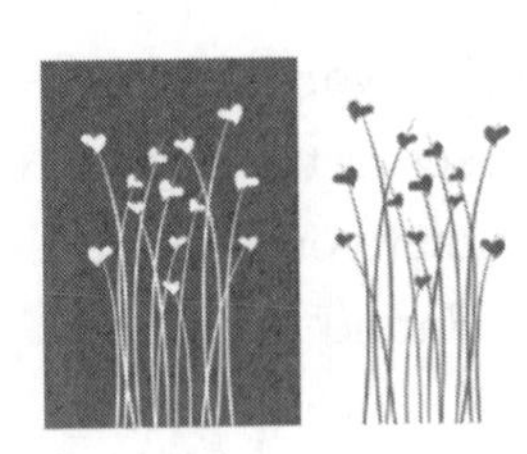

CHAPTER 20

Six months had passed since Hamid had spent 19 days in police custody. The experience left a deep scar in his mind; so deep that he could write comedies but could not bring himself to laugh. He tried to forget but could not. The image of the dark room smelling of foul urine and blood stayed with him. The continuous shouting voices of the policemen, forcing confessions of his crime still rang in his ears. His captivators had tortured him each day and he became a tool for their monstrous and cruel games. There were two men who had been more brutal than the others. One was referred to as "The boxer" as he used Hamid as a punching bag. While the other, Oh God, was "The animal". Sometimes the animal tied him to the table, locked his legs with ropes, secured his feet with his belt and started beating the soles of his feet with his cane. The beating continued until Hamid could no longer feel the pain and fainted. After that he could not walk for days. Flogging, starvation and being deprived to use the toilet were common practice. He contributed to the foul smell of urine and blood in the room. At night he could not sleep and lost the track of time. But all these things were nothing in comparison with the sexual assault. On one occasion the animal took off his clothes and tied him to the table once more. He then tried to penetrate him. Hamid felt hopeless and tried with the little movement he could make to prevent this from happening. The animal smelt of sweat and alcohol. His bottle of vodka was almost empty, but he was still holding it with one hand while trying to direct his penis with the other hand. Fortunately, he collapsed on top of Hamid and fell into a deep slumber. The alcohol saved Hamid. However, he was crushed under the weight of the animal and could not move nor shout for help. The chances were too big that someone else would come to finish the job that the animal couldn't do and rape him. He was occupied with this horrible thought when the animal made a sudden jerking move and dropped the bottle of vodka, which fell on the concrete floor and smashed into pieces. He also fell to the floor with a big bang and made no further sound. Hamid kept quiet.

Three hours later, which seemed like eternity, Hamid finally heard a guard entering the room and shouting: "Guys, call for the ambulance. The bastard killed our colleague with his ass!"

Hamid could hear the nervous steps of the police guards rushing up and down. Finally he was unfastened from the table and given his clothes. It was the biggest embarrassment of Hamid's life and he would have preferred a thousand deaths compared to that situation. A huge amount of blood lay where the animal had fallen.

After that, the animal disappeared. Hamid assumed that he was either dead or in the hospital. Three days later he was released. When he left the gate of the police station, he saw Doctor Nasrat waiting for him. The doctor ran towards him and hugged him.

"Comrade, I'm so happy to see you again," the doctor said.

Hamid could not bear to smile. His spirit and soul had been broken and he could not find anything to say to the doctor. He could not talk about his humiliation at the hands of the policemen.

"You were innocent, Comrade," the doctor comforted him. "They found the man guilty of distributing the *shabnama* just a day after they took you in. He was just an ordinary individual with no relations with our party."

"What? But then why did they keep me locked up so long?" Hamid protested.

"Comrade, this is a corrupt country. Once they take someone into custody, they don't release him easily. If they release someone quickly, it means they had the wrong person. Police in this country never want to admit they are wrong. Once a man is in police custody, he is guilty. You are guilty even if you keep books at home. We should have told you to hide your books," the doctor said.

"No wonder they never interrogated me. Comrade, I suffered so much and want to kill all of them," Hamid said in anger.

"The time will come when the revolutionary court will give you the right to kill them. You will even pull the trigger. Be patient; if you do anything now, you will end up in jail again and we cannot afford losing one of our intelligent comrades," the doctor said.

"I hope I don't die because of depression before that moment comes. To tell you the truth, they are strong and we are not able to get rid of them."

"Don't despair Comrade. Things are happening but slowly. Your release was facilitated by one of our comrades working at the ministry of interior. Right now we have men in the army, in the police department and in ministries. The government is not aware of our network. We are capable of conducting a codetta any time, but our comrades in the Soviet Union will not allow us. They advise us to influence the people to a popular uprising against the government, similar to the Russian Revolution," the doctor said.

"But why? Are they waiting to see more innocent people murdered or tortured? I can't wait," Hamid snapped.

"You must wait, Comrade. By the way, you have been accepted in the faculty of literature. Congratulations, Comrade! Write, write and write. Speed up the revolution with your pen, Comrade," the doctor said.

Hamid was happy but could not smile. He could not even smile six months later when the whole auditorium stormed with laughter. He used his pen as a knife to wound the heart of the government. He knew that Safa and others in the audience could see that his plays were not just for laughs. Safa was not the only one who understood.

CHAPTER 21

It was not the first and last play written by Hamid that Safa read. She developed an amazing thirst for reading Hamid's work. She read his plays, poems and essays and, when she was done, she began reading Russian writers recommended by Hamid. She read Dmitry Merezhkovsky, Maxim Gorky, Alexander Kuprin, Ivan Bunin, Anna Akhmatova, Vladimir Mayakovsky and Sergei Yesenin. Hamid's favourite, Vladimir Mayakovsky, became hers. Sometimes, they read a poem of Mayakovsky together and savoured the poem more. He read one stanza and she the next.

A thousand times over reap of revenge the crops
Never stop!
Petrify, stun,
howl into every ear:
The earth is a convict, hear,
his head half shaved by the sun!

The other thing that they had in common was that they both had wounded hearts, but could not reveal the cause.

It was a never-ending period of unhappiness. Hamid and Safa saw the red colour of revolution in everything. In the green leaves of trees, in the sound of marching comrades, in the chirping of the birds, in the long lines of trees in the jungles, in the gathering of comrades, in the sound of thunder, in the gunshots of comrades on the streets of Kabul, in the patriotic songs and the message of victory.

They felt that the time for revolution to shake their country was near. Safa, like Hamid, was initiated into the party. Their relationship was revolutionary. Two wounded comrades waiting for the revolution to bring equality in their society. They addressed each other as "comrade" and their bond was like that of siblings. Revolution called for blood and they were prepared to sacrifice theirs or to take the blood of their enemies in street encounters. There was blood on the street; plenty of it.

For some time, the government tried to end the freedom of publishing houses, newspapers, magazines and books. The publishing houses, frequently covered by leftist group attacked the government and supported their critique of the social and economic-situation in the country. Banning newspapers was the biggest blow to the leftist movement. They channeled their ideology through newspapers and flyers and were handicapped without a national dissemination media. They felt crippled not being able to communicate to the masses. Hamid was more affected than others. He was the editor as well as a regular contributor to one of those newspapers. Without access to the media he felt trapped and denied of expression. It was as if someone was silencing him and he had a right to have a voice.

In reaction to the government's ban, the People's Party that Hamid belonged to, and other leftist parties, organized a demonstration at the University of Kabul. Many students gathered under the banner of the people's party, but there were also students that belonged to a leftist group supported by China. They referred to themselves as Maoists and occupied the other side of the university. The People's Party gathered in front of the faculty of medicine. Its followers occupied the streets leading to the educational faculties and car parks. Their numbers grew minute by the minute. Red banners were raised with slogans ranging from:

Death to the government;
Death to bloodsucker feudal landowners;
Death to America;
Long live the proletarian movement;
Long live the proletarians of the world;
Long live the Soviet Union, supporter of poor people;
United world the proletariat.

A large Maoist group gathered under white banners in the central park of the university, in front of the library. The same slogans were painted on their banners, but included an additional one: "Long live China" instead of "Long live the Soviet Union." For the first time, the students noticed the gathering of the Muslim Brotherhood party. Although they were small in numbers, they occupied a space adjacent to the people's party. Their appearance was surprising to the leftist groups, because they did not use the press and were not affected by the ban.

The university was filled with an incredible level of noise. Loudspeakers were used to address the audience. The speakers delivered passionate messages and criticised the government. Soon students of nearby schools joined the demonstrations at the university.

They swelled in numbers and there wasn't an unoccupied space. United, the protestors decided to march towards the city. They wanted to express themselves to the nation and not be confined only to university audiences. On the way waves of people joined them under the different banners. Roads were blocked, traffic came to a halt, the noise was deafening, and shopkeepers did not have the choice but to lock up. Innocent onlookers without a real purpose joined the demonstrators. By the time they reached Zarnegar Park, all of Kabul was there. It was chaotic. But Hamid knew that revolutions started with chaos. His heart beat with exhilaration. He had lived to see revolution on the streets of Kabul. Soon these streets would have new owners. They would belong to the people's party, supporters of low class society and the poor people of Afghanistan.

Suddenly, without warning, the Islamic group physically attacked the demonstrators of the People's Party. At that moment the People's Party noticed the presence of the Islamic party. It seemed they purposely came there to attack the People's Party. They were armed with knives and pistols. Soon there was blood on the street: revolution claimed its inevitable victims. Two students were killed and nine others injured. One of the dead students was the only child of his family. The dead and injured were rushed to the hospital. Hamid was not injured, but carried one of his comrades to the nearby hospital. On the way he swore and promised himself that he would not let the enemy of the revolution go unpunished. When his comrade was released from the hospital he came across Safa in the corridor. Safa cried loudly and Hamid fought back his tears.

CHAPTER 22

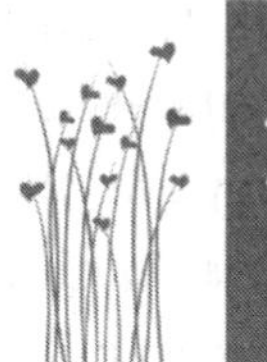

The following day an emergency meeting was held at the People's Party. Hamid noticed the tired and angered expression on the doctor's face. Comrades called for revenge.

The doctor addressed the meeting, "Comrades! The enemy is trying to kill our voice and kill our goal, but we will not let them. I know your immediate reaction is to go ahead and beat the Islamic party followers. Comrades, we should not be diverted from the goal of our party. Our goal is and remains to topple this inhumane government. The Islamic party plays into the hands of this very government."

Hamid was surprised that the doctor advised them not to react, but this was not the doctor's decision. He received orders from his comrades in the Soviet Union, who reiterated the need to stick to the path of revolution without divergence. They wanted the revolution to succeed and were not interested in street fights. Street fights would just give more time to the government before it collapsed.

The government was the real winner of the demonstration. Life was strange indeed. The demonstration had been organized as a protest against the government and yet it had benefited from it. The high officials said: "Let them kill each other! Let them fight each other! One day they will get tired and forget their stupid revolution." But the government was not behind the attack. The Islamic party wanted to leave a historical mark on Afghan politics. For them, the government and the communist parties were both enemies. They were infidels and a *jihad* against infidels was *farz*.

On the surface, a non-reaction to the Islamic party was a sign of maturity and understanding of the situation. Nevertheless, the country and the People's Party were far from understanding the country. Afghanistan was divided between the rich and the poor, between peasants and the city intellectuals. A majority of the people were poor and from rural areas. These people did not have an opinion one way or another about the revolution. How could they? Ninety percent of the demonstrating population did not have access to clean drinking water, electricity, transport, schools or hospitals. Many of them had walked several days and nights to reach Kabul. If one fell sick, he or she was abandoned without aid. That was one of the reasons of infant deaths. Women never made it to hospitals. If they were seriously ill, they were left at home without medical care. Many died from illnesses that could have been easily cured. Revolution only existed in the minds of the leftist groups that were oblivious to what was happening in the rural areas. Hamid was one of them. He could quote from Lenin and Karl Marx, he could recite the poems of Pushkin, he could tell you about the events before the 1917 Russian Revolution, and yet he was not aware of the number of districts in the Bamian province or relate to how people lived there. He had never been outside Kabul or Afghanistan. He judged the country as if all of it was like Kabul. He did not even know the fundamental differences between the Kabul girls wearing miniskirts and the women of the southern provinces not allowed to leave their homes.

After the killing incident, the People's Party issued warnings to its followers to take care and to protect themselves. In the future there would be guards protecting the demonstrators. The party followers were advised not to attack members of other parties, but be prepared to defend themselves. The party was not prepared for the events that unfolded.

The next murder brought the country into turmoil. It was also planned, but the Muslim Brotherhood was not behind it this time. On 19 April 1978 a prominent leftist, Mir Akbar Khyber was assassinated and the murder was blamed on the government. The People's Democratic Party organized a funeral rally as they buried the body of Khyber. On the burial grounds, passionate speeches were delivered by the leaders condemning the government. They accused the government for their alleged hand in the assassination. What they didn't realize at the time were secret agents among them, recording whatever was said against the government. That night homes of the leaders, including the doctor's, were raided and alleged perpetrators imprisoned. Hamid discovered that the doctor was in prison when he heard his name being mentioned on the radio. That night Radio Kabul announced names of traitors and enemies of the country. Hamid decided to go into hiding. With a broken heart he feared that the revolution was defeated. And it was almost true to say that the People's Democratic Party had vanished overnight. The Russians, however, had no intention of allowing this kind of ending. They had worked too hard and for too many years to create the People's Party of Afghanistan. It could not simply disappear overnight.

The government made one vital mistake in their strategy. They kept one prominent leader under house arrest, thinking that he would be immobilised in any case. They lapsed in this badly. His telephone was neither disconnected nor monitored and the leader got a message to the Soviet Union to stage a codetta. The People's Party had enough supporters among the low ranking army officers. They were braver than their seniors and well prepared to take the risk. Soon the air force was under their control. The ground force, loyal to the president, could not move into action without the support of the air force. They were exposed on the ground and bombarded by the air force loyal to the communists. Events moved fast and the presidential palace was attacked. At dawn Kabul witnessed the rising of its new rulers. The president and his family were killed. The Revolution was cruel. The People's Party created a new government. The Soviet Union was the first country to congratulate this new government and recognize its legitimacy.

CHAPTER 23

Revolution is cruel, brutal and sweet, depending on which side you are. For Nasrat and his comrades, such as Hamid, the revolution had a sweet taste. After many years of struggling and fighting, the country was now in the hands of revolutionaries. The new leaders did not waste time announcing the new cabinet. Doctor Nasrat became minister of public health. Hamid headed to his office to congratulate him. When he entered, the doctor jumped out of his chair and gave him a hug.

"Come Comrade Hamid. Didn't I tell you that the day would come when the revolution would succeed and the enemies of the people would be defeated?" the doctor said.

Hamid smiled and sat on one of the chairs. The room was full of people. Every minute a new person came in whom the doctor personally greeted. Hamid had never been in a minister's office before. What a change. Ordinary men came to the office and the minister did not act like someone from another planet. He was just as ordinary as the rest of the people. He thought about these issues when the watchman entered the office and brought three big framed photos with him: one was Taraki, the second was Lenin and the third one was Stalin. Nasrat told the watchman to hang the photos on the wall: Taraki behind him, Lenin on his right and Stalin on his left.

Every now and then a man walked in with a tray of tea and plates full of sweets. The guests drank tea, ate sweets, laughed with joy at the conversation and promised to work hard with the new government to make sure the revolution succeeded. Hamid stayed for a while. He wanted to see happiness on the people's faces.

Before leaving the doctor rose again, gave him a hug and whispered in his ear, "Come to my house this evening. I want to tell you something."

Hamid did not question the purpose of the invitation. He knew that Nasrat did not want to give details in a public office.

On the way home Hamid noticed the presence of red everywhere. The new national flag of Afghanistan was red, huge and hung from the balconies of all public offices. Red banners displayed "Long Live The April Revolution." There were also plenty of national flags of the Soviet Union. Two months later Hamid would hear the joke "Foxes of Kabul would run away while covering their backsides with their tails because wherever the communist party sees a hole, it will put a red flag there." But for now Hamid had no time for silly jokes. He knew that the enemy with silly jokes would disappear one day. He noticed the signs of determination on the faces of soldiers on top of the armoured tanks. People gave them branches of flowers and placed them in the barrel of their machineguns.

In the evening when Hamid was at home, a man came to his house asking for him. He was the doctor's driver. The car was parked on the paved road outside Andrabi. He opened the rear door for Hamid: a habit the driver was accustomed to from serving the previous minister. Hamid told him that it was not necessary and he changed to sit in the passenger seat next to the driver. Hamid thought that the doctor probably changed the venue of their meeting and that was the reason for sending his driver to pick him up. The doctor's house was only a five minute walk to reach.

The car pulled up in front of a big house in a new and fashionable area of Kabul. The driver jumped out to open Hamid's door, but he had already gotten out of the car. He entered a tall gate, crossed a large sized lawn and was guided inside a corridor leading to a back room. From there he could hear the sound of noisy conversation and loud laughter. Once inside his vision was blocked by thick cigarette smoke. He could not see for a few minutes, but heard the familiar voice of the doctor welcoming him.

"Comrade, come here and sit next to me. Time for celebration has come."

Hamid spotted Nasrat. He sat on one of the couches next to a table filled with bottles and glasses. The room was crowded, but Hamid recognised some of the faces of his comrades. The people he did not know were not introduced to him. There was no formality. As soon as he sat down the doctor asked him, "Whisky or vodka?" Hamid was surprised. He never had a drink of alcohol before and it was not because he could not afford it. He did not want to.
The doctor noticed that and said, "Comrade don't worry. It is all right to drink with comrades once in a while. We also need to celebrate and tonight is a good occasion."

"I am not sure Comrade. I have never done this before," Hamid said with hesitation in his voice.

"Comrade, drinking with your revolutionary friends is not wrong."

"Now, tell me which one do you want? The whisky comes from the house of one of our enemies, who cannot drink it anymore because he is in prison. The vodka has been provided by our comrades from the Russian Embassy. The choice is yours."

"Well, if I have to drink, I would prefer to drink the vodka of our comrades."

Hamid started to drink and soon he got used to the bitter taste of vodka and as the evening drew on, an excellent feeling of happiness stole over him and he joined the others in laughter.

After a while he could not trust his ears when the doctor said, "Comrade, you have been appointed as chief editor for our revolutionary newspaper called The Truth. You can occupy your post as of tomorrow. If you need any help you can reach me in my office or at my house. By the way we have also found an apartment for you and you can occupy it whenever you want."

Hamid left after midnight. His head was buzzing and he could not walk straight. The driver helped him to get into the car. On the way home he felt that he probably imagined all the things that had been said in the doctor's house. He thought that was the effect of the alcohol.

The following day he woke up with a message from another driver. He was waiting to take Hamid to his office for his first day on the new job. He now had his own personal car with a driver and a terrible hangover from vodka that he had drunk the night before.

Long live the revolution!

CHAPTER 24

Sitting in his office, Hamid could not believe that the revolution could move so fast. Overnight he had a job that he always dreamed about and with it came a Russian car, a Volga, and as if that was not enough, there was even a flat that belonged to him. It was modern, had two bedrooms and was built by the Russians living in Kabul during the previous president's time. It was large enough for one person but too small for a family. He decided to not to move his parents and Rahmat there because he needed his own privacy now. He wanted to write in his flat without being disturbed by family members and desired to meet his comrades without his family's presence. His comrades had a habit of drinking vodka when they discussed politics and Hamid was sure that his family would not tolerate that.

His office was big and the flow of messages, articles and other printing materials came and went non-stop. He also had the responsibility of contributing to the newspaper. Guidance on how to fill the newspaper came directly from the Soviet Union. Most of the articles were quotes from the new president of Afghanistan, the Soviet Union leader, Karl Marx and Lenin. That made the task of writing easy and difficult at the same time. It was easy because the articles were standard issues and yet it was difficult because no quote could be published with a mistake. Hamid realised that this type of writing did not have any room for imagination. The articles were also sometimes reproduced and his office was responsible to print them on time. His adviser from the Soviet Union wrote and spoke both Persian and Pashto better than many Afghan writers and was responsible for censorship.

Around 4 p.m., when the entire staff left their offices, Hamid finally found spare time for himself and wrote: *Revolution in our beloved country is a very young tree. Young revolutionaries are the gardeners of this tree. They must make sure that they watch this tree with care. There are enemies of this tree who want to cut it. We must make sure that the enemy never gets close to this tree to harm it and if it is necessary, the revolutionaries should give their blood for this tree to grow. This tree does not need water...*

He wanted to write more, but couldn't. He realised that writing a standard article for the revolution was really difficult. It required his imagination to be curtailed and he was not used to it. Unsatisfied, he left the office without taking his car.

After a long walk he reached the university. He waited for Safa to finish her class and when she came out asked: "Fancy a long walk, comrade?" Safa was hesitant and didn't know what to say. It was unusual for her to be in the company of a man walking in the city, but things were changing in Kabul.

"Well, I suppose we could walk towards my house, but when we get close to Andrabi you will have to disappear. I don't want my father seeing me with you."

"Comrade, things are changing for the women of Afghanistan. You have the same rights as I have. You must make an example of yourself. If you cannot walk on the street with your comrade, how can an ordinary Afghan woman, who is not yet liberated by socialist ideas?" Hamid asked.

They walked like two ordinary friends towards Andrabi, where Safa and Hamid's families lived. They took the path leading to Zarnegar Park and saw that Kabul was in a festive mood. The government had ordered the famous singers of Radio Kabul to perform in public to celebrate the victory of the revolution. The park was full of beautiful flowers. The stage had been decorated with the landscape of green hills, covered with grass and flowers and Parasto, a famous female singer sang through the mike:

One rainy night he came to my house,
and filled my room with the fragrance of his body.
It was a rainy night and the rain hit the window's panes
and in the flowerpot of my heart, his love was taking root.

After listening to the song Hamid said, "You know Safa, I have never written a poem of love. I only write poems for the ordinary people."

"Maybe the time has come to write about love, Comrade Hamid. The Revolution has succeeded and now love can grow in your heart," Safa looked at him with a smile.

"The Revolution has just begun Safa and my heart is still full of sorrows. Even the sweet taste of revolution cannot take away my sorrows," Hamid said, avoiding eye contact with Safa.

"Comrade, I am sure that your sorrows are not as deep as mine...," Safa laughed and continued, "Maybe one day we can share our sorrows, but for now I want to share a poem with you."

Ships and -
they have reached the haven.
Trains - also grab to the station.
I am dragged towards you
even faster - because of love.

"Oh wait, wait. Let me read the next stanza," Hamid shouted.

Pushkin's knight is hiding in the basement,
stingy, enjoys his money.

I am coming back
to you, my darling,
My heart is your's.

"Do you remember the end of this poem?" Safa asked.

"Of course, but I let you read it with your beautiful voice."

Admiring, I look
and it washes the darkness,
shaves and bathes.
So do I,
on my way to you,
I am coming back home,
True?
We are reaching final goal.
Terrestrial bond embraces the mortals.
And so,
as soon as we part
You and I,
I firmly aim to you.

"Comrade, Vladimir Mayakovsky is amazing," Hamid said.

"Not as amazing as you Comrade. You are our Vladimir Mayakovsky."

"Please don't exaggerate."

After that Safa disappeared. The park was just a five minute walk from her home.

CHAPTER 25

One Friday afternoon, almost three months after the revolution succeeded, there was a knock on Hamid's door. He put down the novel Jamilya, written by Chingiz Aitmatov, that he was reading and went to answer it. To his surprise it was the doctor, with a bottle of vodka in his hand.

"Would you like to have a drink with me, Comrade?" the doctor asked.

"Salam, Comrade! I am not sure if it is a good time of day to drink."

"Comrade, any time is good to have a drink with me. You know that your friendship is very special to me and I hope it is the same for you."

"Sorry, Comrade, I forgot my manners. Please, come in, this is your home!" Hamid realized that he had not been very hospitable and this was not common for Afghans.

Nasrat sat on the couch and Hamid went to get two glasses with ice. He poured vodka in both glasses and offered one to Hamid.

"Comrade, to your health!"

"To the revolution, Comrade, to the revolution," Hamid said, raising his glass and looking at the doctor's eyes.

They drank one glass after the other. When the bottle was half empty Nasrat said, "Let's drink the rest afterward. We have something to do right now."

Hamid was surprised that the doctor was planning something else on Friday. He wondered if he needed to prepare a written speech for some senior party leader. This was part of his work. The doctor noticed Hamid's wonderment and said, "Don't worry, Comrade. You are not going to do any official work. We are going to shoot targets today." Hamid was even more surprised than before.

Outside the building, the doctor's driver and the bodyguard waited. The bodyguard sat next to the driver and Hamid sat in the back with Nasrat. On the way to their destination Hamid was puzzled by this practical joke. Were they really going target shooting? He had only used a gun once, when one of his friends asked him to join in duck shooting. He did not really enjoy that occasion, especially when he had to leave his bed before sunrise to stand and wait at a pond for the ducks to appear.

Trying to find out what was going on, he said, "Comrade, I hope you are not training me to become a soldier now. You told me that my role was to fight with my pen."

"Comrade, we must be prepared for all possibilities. The people who made the Russian October revolution succeed used both their guns and their pens. Those people will always remain our role models."

"Comrade, when I joined I was prepared to fight with my pen and my gun and I am not scared to lose my life for the revolution," Hamid said, noticing that the doctor was serious about the issue.

"That's the spirit, Comrade. That's the spirit," Nasrat burst into laughter.

The car sped towards the southeastern part of Kabul. Hamid noticed that they were on Jalalabad highway and had travelled a distance of around 20 to 30 kilometers away from the centre of Kabul. The car entered an army post. The watch on Hamid's wrist showed eleven minutes past 4 p.m. and it was still hot. Kabul was always hot in July. Soon the army commander appeared and greeted them.

"Comrade, everything is ready, like you ordered."

"In that case where are the guns?" the doctor asked.

"They are at the target shooting range," the commander replied.

"Excellent, I can't wait," the doctor said.

Hamid was nervous. What was all this about? He was aware that some comrades took shooting lessons, but those were well planned and not like this. An army jeep picked them up and brought them to the shooting range. In the distance Hamid could see five standing oil barrels.

Nasrat realized that Hamid had seen the barrels and said, "Today we'll start with easy targets. We will just shoot those five barrels." Then he faced the commander, and said, "I still don't see the guns."

Two Kalashnikovs were brought: one for the doctor and the other for Hamid. The commander taught them how to use the guns and soon they were shooting the barrels. Each time the bullets hit the barrels, Hamid shouted with joy.

Nasrat shouted too, "Hit the target, Comrade. Think of the enemy." When they finished their rounds of bullets, Hamid handed his gun to the commander and walked toward the jeep. He was about to leave the army compound but Nasrat stopped him.

"What's the hurry, Comrade? Now we must see how many bullets hit the target."

Hamid walked back to the barrels with the doctor. When they stood in front of the barrels, the doctor looked inside of one of them.

"Comrade, the real target is inside."

Hamid looked inside and to his horror saw a dead man in each barrel. They wore police uniforms and their mouths were shut with tape.

"This is the animal, Comrade. The one who tortured you day after day," shouted the doctor.

Hamid looked inside the barrel that Nasrat was pointing at and saw a dead body hit by so many bullets in the face that it was unrecognizable. Hamid was initially paralysed and could not move. He noticed that his heartbeat had quickened and that his hand trembled. Without knowing what he was doing, he reached inside the barrel and touched the face of the man who was supposed to be the animal. He wanted to remember the face of the man who nearly raped him.

They went back to Hamid's flat to finish the other half of the vodka bottle. Before leaving Nasrat raised his last glass, "Here is to the revolution, Comrade. The Revolution never forgets its enemies." The policeman nicknamed the animal and his friends were not innocent, but the speed of punishing guilty people after the revolution was beyond imagination. Comrades were permitted to take decisions by themselves and killed the so-called guilty. Radio Kabul always announced the revolutionary court of justice and yet no one saw this court. People were prosecuted without evidence or trial. Khad, the national security service was mainly blamed for killing and imprisonment of the people. Khad was modeled according to the KGB and had many advisors from Russia. The person in charge of Kahd was a man named Alam. He had a very short fuse and did not hesitate to pull the trigger whenever he wanted. The name Alam brought terror to the people of Kabul.

CHAPTER 26

It was raining. Mullah Rabani had just finished his *zohar* lunch time prayers. Not many people turned up for the *namaz,* only the five followers. He was aware, given the bad weather that the number of worshipers frequenting the mosque decreased. But what particularly bothered him was that he did not see Rahmat among the worshipers. No matter what, Rahmat always attended the afternoon prayers and even stayed on thereafter to continue his Islamic studies with Mullah Rabani. Must be the rain, Rabani assumed; however, instead of returning to his room he sat in the mosque. He picked up a book to read. More than half an hour later while reading he was interrupted by Rahmat's voice.

"*Salam* Mullah Sahib."

"Must be the rain, ha? Don't worry, the whole of Andrabi is scared of rain and not many came to worship God this afternoon," Rabani said and smiled reassuringly.

"No it wasn't the rain, Mullah Sahib; I wish it had been as simple as the rain."

"Don't tell me, you are not feeling well?"

"No, I am not feeling well," Rahmat said without explanation.

"Are you sick? Tell me. Do you need to see a doctor?"

"No I am not sick," Rahmat continued in riddles.

"Rahmat what is the problem then?" Rabani asked impatiently.

"I am late because of Alam."

"Why? Was he suspecting something?"

"Not me, Mullah Sahib. He came after Munir, our neighbour."

"That quiet boy who attends the mosque?"

"Yes."

"Did Alam take him away?"

"Not him, his brother," Rahmat continued his riddles.

"Rahmat I am really puzzled. You first talk about Munir and then you switch to his brother. Are you all right?"

"Mullah Sahib Alam came for Munir, but Munir had already disappeared. I suppose he knew that Alam would come after him. His brother Kasem told me some days back Munir had made a grave mistake criticising the government in public. Since then we have not seen Munir. When Alam came in search he was in a bad mood. Accompanied with the police they thoroughly searched the house for Munir. When it became evident that Munir was nowhere to be found, he became very angry. He then questioned the family, but the family knew no more of his disappearance. At that point Alam became wild and started beating Kasem to obtain a confession on Munir's whereabouts. Kasem repeated that he did not know Munir's whereabouts. Alam then ordered the police to take Kasem into custody, until Munir gave himself up. It has been two days now and yet no one knows where Kasem is being held. Today I went with his father to the police station because Kasem is a good friend of mine. We are of the same age and grew up together here in Andrabi. The police refused to cooperate, but finally mentioned that only Mr. Alam would know where he is held. I am really worried for Kasem and his family. His parents are elderly. They have two sons and five daughters. Now both their sons have disappeared and the mother is crying, day and night!"

"I am sorry to hear this. This infidel government has no mercy."

"All we want is to find out where Kasem is. His mother wants to send food and clean clothes for him."

"Leave it to me. I will find out."

"What do you mean Mullah Sahib?"

"I have some contacts."

"Contacts?" Rahmat was surprised.

"I know about Alam very well. I even know some of his personal life details. I know for instance that the woman he married had been previously engaged to another. In fact, Alam had her fiancé imprisoned and threatened her family with the same if they tried to stop Alam's marriage to her. They had no choice, but to agree."

"Oh Mullah Sahib you never told me this before."

"It is a matter of trust and secrecy. By telling you this tale now I endanger my own life! You know, not all the secret police staff are infidels. There are some God fearing people who work for Khad simply because they have family to feed. It is these people who inform me on occasion what is going on. Please tell no one what you have heard today. I will find out about your friend. But the information I give you, never reveal the source, at any cost!"

Rahmat was very excited of the possibility to learn of his friend's fate and also because Rabani had entrusted him with his life. He said, "My lips are sealed Mullah Sahib and thank you for trusting me."

"Rahmat I know that you are trustworthy. Now I have to prepare the mosque for the *aser*, late afternoon prayers. I will give you the news as soon as I can find out."

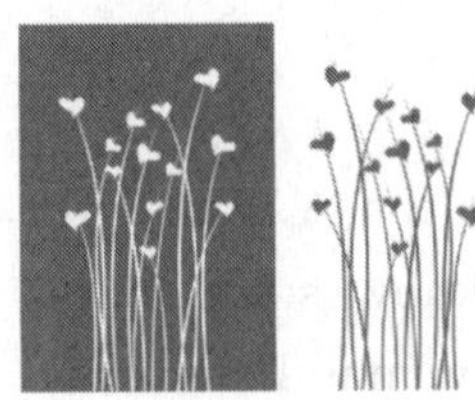

CHAPTER 27

The *maghrib,* evening prayers finished. The mosque this time had been filled. In the evenings people came to the mosque after work. It was two days since Rabani's conversation with Rahmat on Kasem. Rahmat was about to depart for home when Rabani caught up with him.

"Rahmat wait, I have something to tell," Rabani said.

"Okay," Rahmat stopped his steps waiting for the mullah to speak further. However, Rabani kept quiet and indicated with his eyes that too many people were still around. Rahmat sat down on the mosque floor, pretending to pray, while inwardly Rabani was truly reciting the one hundred names of God, silently, again and again, until the last of the worshiper had left the mosque premises.

"I have information about your friend Kasem," Rabani finally broke the silence.

"Praise Allah what is it? His family would be so happy."

"I don't know how to tell you Rahmat," Rabani's voice filled with concern and sadness.

"What is it Mullah Sahib?" asked Rahmat.

"It is not easy," Rabani sighed.

"What happened?" He persisted in knowing despite the apprehension of fear now.

"That day when Alam came for Munir, he took Kasem in his car. On the way Alam started swearing and cursing Munir's family. Alam kept telling Kasem that he was a bastard and his brother was the son of a whore too. At one point Kasem swore back at Alam. In a matter of seconds, Alam took out his pistol, put it into Kasem's mouth and fired the gun. After that, he asked his driver to get off on the street and himself drove to a place outside Kabul to get rid of the body.

"Oh God no! How did you find out?" Rahmat asked.

"The man in the car informed me."

"You mean, the driver?"

"Yes he is my informant," Rabani admitted.

"How am I going to tell his family of this?"

"I told you it would not be easy. Now you can appreciate that the driver is an informant. You must know that his whole family could be wiped out if Alam ever finds out."

"Oh God!"

"So better not to say anything for their sake."

"What a country!"

"It is a country in the hands of infidels, Rahmat."

"Allah please help me. Now that I know about what happened to Kasem, it is far too horrible, I cannot possibly share it with his family."

"No you can't. Remember you would destroy the life of the driver and his family if you do."

A week later, Alam's driver left the Khad's service in a dramatic way. He had actually wanted to leave Alam's service immediately on that awful night, but had some plan to carry out first. The same driver regularly informed the resistance fighters called Mujahidin about the terrors of Alam.

What Rabani did not know was that Khad was also gathering information about him. Through their investigation, Khad found out that Rabani had a hand in the killings of the People's Party activists during the demonstration before the revolution.

One summer night shortly past midnight, there was a knock on the door of the mosque. Rabani came out of his room and talked with a man who introduced himself as working for the Khad. They were inside the mosque for about ten minutes before Rabani accompanied him. The man had come with the same car that belonged to Alam. He was Alam's driver. In the car, the driver overheard a conversation between Alam and one of his comrades about capturing Rabani for the killing of the students. For many months, the driver planned his exit from the Khad. He worked for them out of necessity, not by choice. He knew that Mullah Rabani and himself were religious men. Alam planned to capture Rabani the following night, but the driver intercepted with a daring move. He dropped off his boss and went to see Rabani at the mosque. He was able to drive the mullah to a safe place in the middle of the night without being challenged by guards at the checkpoints. A week earlier he had sent all his close family members to Pakistan. The following day he left Kabul with Rabani and headed to Pakistan after abandoning the car in an empty street.

Eight months after the April revolution it was the Muslim Brotherhood who gained strength day by day. They also called themselves Mujahidin. They had penetrated the army, the police and even the Khad. Alam's driver was one of Rabani's men and yet he was only a driver. Rabani had many men working in senior positions for the army and the police. Desertion from the army and the police soon became common. These same men would have left the army and the police anyway with their weapons and used them against the communist regime. Their base was in Pakistan and Iran. The Pakistani government, Iran, USA, China and the Arab countries all supported the Mujahidin cause. For the Americans the Mujahidin were soldiers fighting the Russians and they would bring them down just like Americans were defeated in Vietnam. Afghanistan became a playground for wars and politics.

When Alam discovered Rabani's implication of the killings before the revolution Rabani realised that his plans were in jeopardy. He had been happy secretly leading and directing his Mujahidin from the small mosque. He was accepted as their leader and had contacts with resistance fighters in Afghanistan as well as in Pakistan. Messages were received and sent in coded language and sent back to fighters all over the country. For him the mosque was the best place to direct his activities. But now he had no other option but to leave Andrabi.

The house where Rabani spent the night was far away from the centre of Kabul. It was a hiding place that the Mujahidin used for their operations. Not somewhere to send fighters to face the Russians or the Afghan government soldiers, but a place of communication with Mujahidin. This house was the first stop for eager men to be recruited and become a mujahid. Most of the people were sent from this house to Pakistan to get weapons and come back to Afghanistan to fight the government. These communication houses were established all over the country but this one was the most important because it was located near Kabul and under Rabani's observation. He had been in this house many times since the government had changed. In fact, he had initiated houses like this all over the country.

Getting Rabani out of Kabul and bringing him to Pakistan was not an easy task. If he was captured, the Mujahidin would lose their leader as well as their entire system of communication. It would not be that simple to replace Rabani. The mullah had contacts with the Arabs, the Pakistani government and even the west. It was amazing that the Afghan government and its KGB allies did not discover what Rabani was secretly doing in Kabul. He had an impressive ability of hiding his activities and acting innocent.

To accomplish this mission, five men were involved to take their leader to Pakistan. They travelled in pairs: two men in the front, two men in the back and Rabani in the middle with one man. Since the house was on the outskirts of Kabul, there was no danger of being searched at the checkpoints. It would have been extremely dangerous if they had been stopped and searched since there were many checkpoints on the highway to Pakistan. Rabani and his men did not take the risk of travelling by private car, taxi or bus. They began their journey on foot and it would take them five days and nights.

They mostly travelled at night, under the cover of darkness, and chose a path that was not used by government soldiers. The government had sent fighters to all corners of Afghanistan since the entire country was at war with them. The most dangerous weapon they had were Russian helicopter gunships. The pilots using these gunships were well trained to spot the Mujahidin or other suspected groups from a great distance and bombard them. Night was the only safe travel time. But even then, the government deployed troops of helicopters on the hillside where soldiers hid in the dark watching for movement. People traveling at night were suspects because they had chosen to hide themselves in the darkness.

All the way to the border of Pakistan, Rabani witnessed the marks of war. When they entered a village they could not see any sign of humans. Destroyed houses were abundant.

"Allah, have mercy on us. They have left their homes in fear of being bombed," Rabani said.

"Toba Allah, toba," one of the men said.

Rabani was shocked and sat on the ground. His knees could not support his weight anymore.

"They have destroyed the house of Allah," he said, pointing to a mosque with a collapsed roof and demolished walls.

"We pray in this destroyed house of Allah and pray for their destruction, brothers."

They performed *namaz* on the rubble and dust. No one spread *jainamaz,* the praying rug since everything was clean in their mind. This was the house of Allah and touching its dust with their forehead made them feel humble as well as make them aware that as long as the enemy was ruling their homeland, Muslims would be humiliated.

After the *namaz,* Rabani heard a voice originating from the entrance of the ruins. "My brother once lived in this village," a man with a long grey beard, wearing a dirty white turban said.

"What?" Rabani asked surprised, getting up from his praying position.

"That was the house of my brother," the man pointed towards a destroyed house in ruins.

"Where is your brother now?" one of the men accompanying Rabani asked.

"He is in a mental hospital in Peshawar."

"He went mad because he lost his home?" Rabani asked.

"No."

"Then what happened?"

"It is a long story."

"We have time. Tell us man what happened?" Rabani asked patiently.

"It was the end of summer. I was visiting my brother's land at the time to help him with his harvest. Suddenly from nowhere, Mujahidin appeared. They took position in a ditch not far from our village and started shooting at the government post. It was out there. Can you see it?" The man was pointing to a fort built of mud some 2 kilometres in the distance

"Yes I see it." Rabani replied

"The government responded with heavy weapons, tanks and machine guns. The place became a war zone within minutes. My brother and I also took cover in a nearby ditch, praying for the fight to be over. But no, the war intensified minute by minute. We could not return while in the middle of the battle ground. If we had left the ditch we certainly would have been killed instantly in the crossfire, either by the Mujahidin's bullets or the government's. So we stayed put. Night fell and in the cover of the darkness the Mujahidin disappeared one by one. While there was no longer rocket fire or gunshots from the Mujahidin's position, yet the government continued shelling the village, despatching more planes to bomb too. Finally at daylight, the government stopped firing, noticing then that the enemy had fled. We also headed back to our homes to look for our families; but then I wished my brother had also died in that shooting."

"What are you implying, man? What happened?" Rabani appeared shocked.

"Yes, it would have been better if he had died because what unfolded was much worse than a dead man's fate. We first went to his home. Nothing was left of the house. There was no roof and no walls that were undamaged. My brother was shocked at this sight and screamed for his sons, 'Osman, Osman where are you? Najib can you hear me where are you? Fatima, Raihan'. But there was no sign of his sons, neither his wife, Fatima, nor his daughter, Raihan.

We started digging the debris with our hands in fear. Soon other neighbours came with spades to assist. We dug frantically. Finally we found the body of Raihan without her head and half the body of Fatima. My brother grabbed the dirt with his fist and threw it on his head screaming. His cry could be heard miles away. We searched for ages, but could not find the body of the boys. The kind villagers did not give up. They continued digging until night fell and then brought hurricane lamps and continued digging.

I took my brother to my house. Fortunately, as luck would have it, in contrast my home was not damaged. The whole night I could hear my brother's wailing. In the morning the villagers confirmed that they had found nothing more. It was at that point that my brother clung to the hope that maybe the boys had run away when the fight broke out and were too frightened to return. A day thereafter, a boy climbed a nearby tree. You see that big chenar tree there?" the man pointed towards a tree. The boy found Osman's shirt with some of his flesh. As for Najib, he is still missing. Some people prefer to believe that he might have been taken by the Mujahidin to a safe place. But I don't believe in anything. A month later my brother went quite mad. We admitted him to a mental hospital."

"Oh Allah, have a mercy on us. You still live here?" Rabani asked.

"No, the entire villagers left. I only returned to check on the house. You see our refugee camp is on the border and it is easy for me to return to our village, half a day's walking distance from there. Until four months ago my house had not been hit by bombs, but today it too has been destroyed."

"This is dangerous ground, this village," Rabani said.

"Yes. Only two kilometres away from the government post. It provides a good position for the Mujahidin. They always fight from here. The Mujahidin plan to take over the government post one day."

They past barren farm land and crossed a bridge that was half destroyed. On the other side of the village they saw a group of Mujahidin. They seemed fearless and determined to go to war against the government, who had the full support of the Soviet Union and was regularly provided with the most modern weapons of the time.

On the way there were no more houses to spend the night. Rabani's men could not trust anyone. When people are at war, they change sides easily. The government bribed many people in the villages to become spies for the government. They would report back what the Mujahidin were up to. Rabani and his men slept under the marvellous sky, full of stars. They listened to the sound of streams at night and despite excessive tiredness managed to get some rest.

The food they carried was simple bread, hard and old. Fortunately for them there were many fruit trees on the way.

After five days and nights, with little food and rest, Rabani and his men reached Pakistan. He was happy when he discovered that a huge building was assigned to him to use as his house and office. The Pakistan government and the Arabs who supported *jihad* in Afghanistan provided this building for the leader of the Mujahidin. Rabani also discovered that he had a car and driver.

In his heart he thanked the revolution, which gave him such opportunity. Otherwise, he would have remained a simple mullah. The Revolution made the People's Party leaders rich, just like it made the leader of the Mujahidin rich, but destroyed the life of ordinary people.

Yet both sides claimed to fight for the cause of the people.

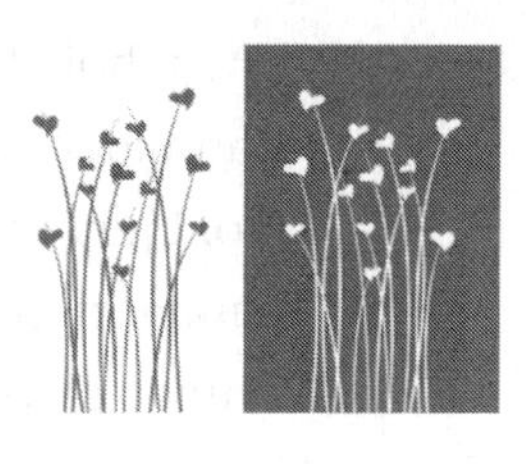

CHAPTER 28

Rahmat had been waiting for Hamid for many hours. When he finally arrived, Rahmat ran towards him and give him a tight hug as if he had not seen his brother for many years.

"What is it Rahmat?" Hamid asked surprised.

"You haven't heard?"

"Of course I heard. That is the reason that I am late. We had an emergency meeting."

Hamid pretended to be surprised to see Rahmat. In the meeting the comrades had decided that they would remain calm and pretend that nothing had happened.

That afternoon there was a huge explosion in the ministry of education not far from Andrabi. The explosion destroyed half of the second floor of the building and caused many deaths and injuries. It was like an earthquake, shattering the windows. Hamid's mother was alone at home when the incident happened. The first thing she thought of was the safety of her children. The news reached Rahmat quickly and he came home as soon as he could. His mother was delighted to see that he was safe and urged him to contact his brother. Rahmat tried to phone but the lines were cut, perhaps from the explosion. He left home and tried to take a bus to Hamid's office, but there were no buses plying in the city. Finding no transport, he walked for hours until he reached his brother's office, only to find that it was closed and no one could give him any news about his whereabouts. Rahmat could not go back to his mother unless he knew what had happened. He continued walking for many hours until he reached Hamid's flat.

"The whole family is worried sick," Rahmat said.

"Rahmat, come inside."

"No, I just wanted to see if you were safe."

"I am very tired and you must be too. Come."

Rahmat stepped in, but had no desire to stay. He sat on a chair and counted the minutes until he could go back home. Hamid looked very tired. The explosion was the first of its kind to shake the capital. These things usually only happened in the provinces and in the countryside. The government was shocked and had asked its key cadres to meet immediately. Hamid belonged to that group.

"This is the work of our enemy, Rahmat."

"What enemy?"

"Are you joking with me?"

"Hamid, I don't know anything about politics."

"That is exactly what is wrong with you. I am amazed to have managed to enrol thousands of people into our party but had no influence on you."

Hamid took out his frustration on Rahmat without noticing. Tiredness and fear made him less sensitive towards his brother.

"I'm sorry Rahmat. It's been a terrible day. Do you want a drink of water?"

"Yes."

"You know I never imagined what the enemy could do in Kabul," Hamid said, handing a glass of water to Rahmat.

"I suppose our life has changed forever now."

"Rahmat, we need people to support us. You must join us. You know that I won't put pressure on you. Do you ever read my articles? The enemy is destroying our country. Two days ago they burned seven schools and three government buildings in Parwan. They are against education and against progress."

"Yes, I have read all these things in your newspaper."

"And yet you haven't decided to join us?"

"I also heard about Herat."

"What about Herat?"

"Thirty thousand people were killed by Russians."

"Hey, do you believe the enemy's propaganda? Don't you trust your brother?"

"I don't know. I suppose they are all stories."

"Of course, you don't know, idiot."

"At least, you could have informed us about your safety; so I would not have had to come and bother you with my stupidity."

"I have to think about the country Rahmat, the country," Hamid was shouting.

"And what about your family?"

"My family is part of this country."

"I have to go now. Mother must be worried."

"How can you leave when there is a curfew?"

"I cannot let mother worry."

"I'll take you home."

"That would be good. Mother would be relieved to see you safe."

"Rahmat, there is a revolution going on."

"I know Hamid, and we are all in it."

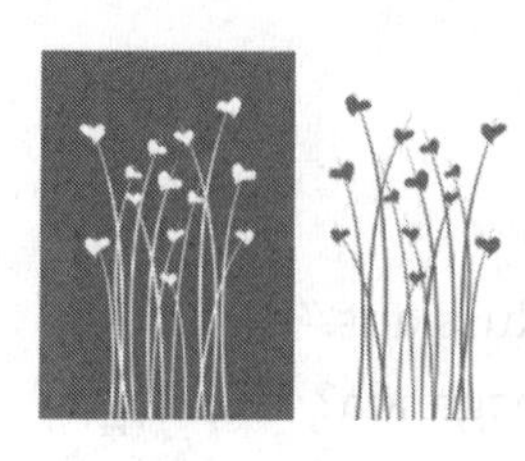

CHAPTER 29

God had created two different worlds in two neighbouring countries. The difference between Afghanistan and Iran was obvious. Tehran, the capital of Iran, was a very busy city. It was modern with wide boulevards, new cars, sophisticated public transport, five star hotels, big parks full of beautiful flowers and fountains. It had amazing shopping centers with goods from all over the world. Young people were fashionable and bought their clothes from shops that had brands from Rome, Paris and London. Girls' faces appeared on the back of glossy magazines. There were at least five magazines dedicated to women and each one competed with the other. The cover of each magazine had the image of a beautiful woman. There were beautiful women everywhere: on the streets, in the parks, in the restaurants, in the nightclubs, in the bars; and on the silver screen some even showed their half naked bodies. It was the time of the miniskirt revolution, which Iranians referred to it as mini jupe, using the French word. Tehran was greatly influenced by the French language and the French culture. The young people loved the time they were living in. Bars openly served alcohol and when young men got drunk, they found comfort in the arms of wives or girlfriends; and if they had none there were plenty of prostitutes. Tehran was both heaven and hell. It was heaven for young Iranians and it was hell for young Afghan men who came there in search of work.

Everywhere there were marks of an Afghan hard at work. Modern houses, parks, roads, factories, schools, hospitals, cinemas, new cars, bicycles were the work of Afghan men. They were often used and abused. They were the only ones desperate enough to take on any type of job and there were plenty of jobs for desperate men. These were tough jobs and Iranians were not prepared to do them. There was too much oil money and Iranians were rich. Rich men were not made for hard work.

Golo enjoyed his first month in Tehran. He had some money to use to go out and see the beauty of the city while his friends were busy working. The flat that he shared with his friend was, in fact, only one bedroom, with a kitchen in a corner and a shared toilet located outside. Golo and his friend were not the only ones in that tiny flat: there were other migrant workers. Three people lived in the tiny space: Golo, his friend and a colleague of his friend. There was hardly any space for them to sleep and yet it was Afghan custom to tolerate guests, especially if they were close friends. Golo used this kindness for his benefit.

When his money was used up, he borrowed from his friend until his friend politely said that he did not have any more to give him. At that point Golo realized that he didn't even have money to go back to Kabul. Finally, he decided find a job like many other Afghans. He would be working for the first time and it would be tough. The only job that he could get was as a labourer in building projects, since he had no qualifications or experience. His friend, on the other hand, was an experienced electrician and worked in an electrical appliance factory.

The time had come for Golo to leave his paradise. He could not take the pressure anymore and he was also embarrassed. How could he face his father and how could he face Safa? As a sign of kindness, Golo's friend decided to introduce him to his boss. He would inquire if a job could be found that did not require specific qualifications. It was not easy to make an appointment with the boss, but in a stroke of luck he agreed to meet Golo.

That morning Golo wore clean clothes and accompanied his friend to his boss' office. When they arrived the secretary informed them that the boss had not arrived yet. His friend left for work and left Golo behind waiting. An hour later a Mercedes arrived and someone rushed to open the front door for the driver. The driver was no other than the boss of the company, dressed in an immaculate suit and sunglasses. He was in his thirties and looked handsome. When he reached the entrance of his office, Golo rushed to open the door for him. The boss glanced at him and Golo just managed to mention that his friend had informed him about the possibility of a job. The boss did not reply and went inside. After a long time, Golo was asked to enter the office. He noticed that his heart was beating fast and that his throat was dry.
He only managed to say, "Salam," to which the boss did not reply.

"What do you want?" The boss asked.

"Sir, my friend said that there might be a possibility of getting a job in your company," Golo replied.

"Are you an electrician?" the boss asked.

"No Sir," Golo answered, embarrassed.

"But I only employ electricians," the boss said impatiently.

"Sir, I could do any simple job you ask. I just don't have any experience or qualification," Golo begged him.

A long pause followed and killing silence settled over the room. Golo expected the boss to ask him to leave the office, but he didn't. Instead he looked out of the window for a long time, contemplating. Golo could study the left profile of his face clearly without the boss being aware. Golo observed him closely. His eyes were that of an aristocrat. His long eyelashes could be seen from the distance where Golo was standing. The eyes didn't necessarily indicate whether he was kind or cruel, they just showed beauty. Golo remembered his mother saying that men who have large foreheads are bound to be lucky. The boss had a large forehead and, indeed, he seemed lucky. The large forehead did not show signs of hair loss. His hair style was unique. The long drawn out silence gave Golo an opportunity to think of where he had seen a similar hair style. He recalled a similar one belonged to Alain Delon, the famous French actor in the film *The Motorcycle*, which he had seen only two weeks ago.

He kept looking at him. At last, he said, "Do you know how to drive?"

Golo's eyes sparkled and he immediately said, "Yes."

"Well, in that case wait for me outside the office. I will leave in two hours and you will drive me. I will test your driving abilities."

Testing Golo was just a matter of formality. He was an experienced driver, but maybe the boss wanted to make sure that Golo was capable of driving in Tehran. Tehran was much bigger and had heavier, unruly traffic in comparison to Kabul. Golo easily passed the test and felt extremely lucky to have been employed as the boss' personal driver without any qualifications. Actually the boss had been looking for someone for a long time. His previous driver had left to go back to his village after losing his wife. Work as a driver seemed like a better and cleaner job than anything else Golo had done before in Tehran. He was even offered a good salary and given a room next to the watchman of the house. The room was luxurious compared to the small dirty flat that he shared with the other two Afghans. The boss' house was like a palace. The garden was enormous and two gardeners were employed to look after it. Iranians referred to such houses as villas. This one was three stories high and big enough for a king.

As the time passed, Golo realized that the boss was happy with his work. He drove the car with care, kept it clean, never spoke unless he was asked and tried his best to be polite. It appeared that he was quite suitable for this kind of job. Being poor in Tehran forced Golo to change completely.

Mr. Jamshid, better known as the boss, was no ordinary man. He was the son of the finance minister, who was related to the queen. Since the minister was a relative of the royal family, he always retained his ministerial post in any cabinet. No one questioned how it was possible that he could be minister of culture once, minister of commerce another time and later minister of finance. Not including him in the cabinet would have been an insult to the queen. The minister was probably one of the richest men of Iran. All of his wealth was inherited. The same wealth would be passed on to his two children: a daughter and a son.

Jamshid was actually an artist. Looking after the factories was his father's idea. His father did not believe in art. Firstly, his son was not the best painter, and secondly, even if he was a talented painter, no one in Iran was going to pay him enough to live from this profession. Art was not considered to be a profitable business in Iran. According to his father, Jamshid had enough time in the past for painting and other activities. He agreed to paint only in his spare time and manage his father's factories and land fulltime. Being in his late thirties, he was now more realistic about his future in Iran as a painter. He had learned art in Paris for 10 years. In Paris, he learned to live like a free spirited artist knowing no barrier in expressing his feelings.

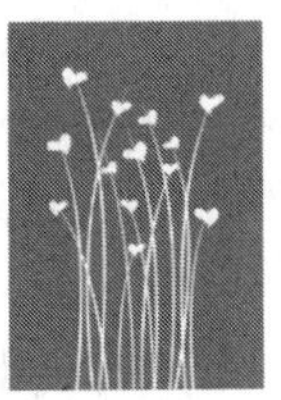

CHAPTER 30

Golo and the two gardeners watched TV in his room on a black and white set provided by Mr. Jamshid, when they were interrupted by the cook: "Mr. Jamshid wants to talk to you," he urged. Golo immediately got up. In the past the cook would regularly beckon him to get the car ready at the boss' request. But this time he was asked to come to the main house. His heart started beating fast. It must be an important matter, he thought. Perhaps he does not like my style of driving.

Two days ago he had momentarily forgotten that he was on a driving assignment. In a state of absent-mindedness, he occasionally took his eyes off the road, relaxed with only one hand on the wheel, watched the pedestrians and other things on the roadside. Jamshid noticed the lapse and told him to be more careful and not to drive so fast. Golo immediately corrected himself and had been on his best behaviour the next day. The night following his lapse he couldn't sleep, cursing himself for his mistake. Perhaps, he was being called to be punished. The possibility of losing his job crossed his mind. The distance between his room and the main house had never seemed so long. He followed the cook into the main hallway. It was a wide and decked with a beautiful Persian carpet. Golo took his shoes off at the entrance and continued to follow the cook, observing the objects on the walls. The walls were enriched with priceless paintings and extravagantly framed family photographs. Several semi circular, elegantly ornamented tables were decorated with fresh and vibrant flower bouquets.

The wide corridor led to a larger circular hall with an overpowering central chandelier and fashionable furniture, probably all imported from Europe. Golo followed the cook and climbed up a wide marble staircase in the centre of the house. On the first floor they turned right. At the third door, the cook paused to check that Golo was still behind him before knocking, on what he later learned to be Mr. Jamshid's study.

When they heard the response "Enter!" the cook opened the door, but stayed near the doorway. "*Salam* Sir, the driver is here," he announced.

Mr. Jamshid glanced at him from behind his desk. He browsed what seemed to be a recent book on Italian paintings. The cook left and Mr. Jamshid went back to his book, leaving Golo standing, frozen in the doorway.

After what seemed like an eternity, Jamshid said: "Shut the door and come closer!"
Golo took some unconfident steps towards Mr. Jamshid and stopped halfway.

"Come closer," Mr. Jamshid said impatiently. "I want to ask you to do something for me, but first I must be absolutely sure that I can trust you."

Jamshid looked directly into Golo's eyes. Golo couldn't say anything. He was speechless. Silence filled the room. What could such an influential person want from him, a poor refugee from Afghanistan, who couldn't even find a qualified job?

"Did you hear what I said?"

"Yes Sir, of course. You can trust me. I owe you my life."

"Are you sure that I can trust you?"

"Sir, with all my life."

"Well, if I tell you what I want and you don't keep your promise, you will lose your life. It is easy for me to get rid of people like you, you know. "

"I know Sir, but you can trust me. I am your loyal servant. "

"In that case, I want you to find me some opium from your Afghan contacts. Never mention that I have asked for it. I need it for Friday afternoon. Do you think you'll be able to find some? Here take this money," he said, offering Golo a bunch of notes.

Golo was relieved. He had expected much worse. In his life he never consumed opium before, but was aware that many Afghans traded opium in Tehran. There was a good possibility that his Afghan friend knew someone who did. Opium was the drug of the rich and intellectuals of Tehran. They consumed it to prove their intellect and to show off their wealth. Jamshid was both rich and intellectual; so he was more qualified than others to indulge in this type of vice.

The following day, after dropping off his boss at work, he asked for permission to search for what Jamshid had requested. He did not mention what it was, which was part of their secret.

By Thursday Golo was a proud man. The world seemed like his oyster: luck was smiling down at him. He hadn't imagined that his boss would confide in him so quickly. He was surprised to find out that it was not too difficult to get opium and enough to keep his boss and his company happy for a long time. Besides he was left with considerable amount of money to return. In normal circumstances he would have simply kept the money for himself, but he was wise enough to know that this was not the time for such games. He wanted to ensure that his boss trusted him in future. The previous thief was becoming an honest man, at least in this instance. He kept the opium and the money on him and waited for the boss to enquire about his mission. He did not wish to bother Mr. Jamshid. Friday would come when he would present the opium to him. There was no need to rush it.

On Friday Golo counted the minutes to be asked about his mission. Around 3 pm, Mr. Jamshid asked for his car to leave the office. Once seated, Jamshid enquired about the opium. Golo proudly handed the opium and the remaining money. He had already started driving towards the house when Jamshid informed him that he was not going home. He gave him directions to head south of Tehran instead.

They reached a villa just before sunset, driving along a scenic road. Golo stopped in front of large grey iron gates and beeped his horn. An elderly watchman opened the gate and gave Jamshid a formal salutation. It was one of Jamshid's villas, situated in one of the most beautiful parts of the country, famous for its natural beauty. When Jamshid visited, it was not only to admire the scenery. He threw wild parties in the isolated villa surrounded by extensive land. It was completely private. Guests swam in the pool, walked in the garden practically naked, listened to the music in the moonlight, danced and drank. The servants were forbidden to mention any of these activities to outsiders. Jamshid relied on their agreement in keeping his private life secret.

He entered the villa followed by Golo, carrying his briefcase. As usual, he carried the briefcase to the entrance of Jamshid's destination, but Golo never went further than that. This time, however, Jamshid specifically asked him to follow. He complied and observed that the villa was as grand as Mr. Jamshid's house in Tehran. They entered an impressive hall where Jamshid told him to sit down. It was the first time that Golo sat in the company of Jamshid. He hesitated at first, thinking that he must have misheard. But when he was firmly told to sit down again, he chose a chair instead of the comfortable sofa and sat on the edge of it. His surprise changed to shock when his boss asked him if he wanted to join him for a drink.

Golo could not answer and Jamshid did not ask again. He simply went to the bar and poured whiskey – his favourite drink in two crystal glasses and handed one to Golo. Golo stood up as he accepted the glass as a sign of respect, but before he could sit down on the chair again, Jamshid gestured for him to sit on a nearby sofa instead. Golo became very tense and did not enjoy the moment, given the circumstances. In the past the thought of having a glass of whiskey with his boss would have brought a big smile on his face. He was not worried getting drunk with his friends, but scared of what would happen if he drank too much in front of the boss whom he greatly feared. He felt itchy and before realising he had finished his drink. Using this as an opportunity, he requested to take leave, but Jamshid told him not to be in a hurry and poured him another glass of whiskey.

The second glass of whiskey went straight to Golo's head. He began to loosen up and forget his shyness. By the time food was served, he accepted Jamshid's offer to join him at the table. The food was delicious, the best that Golo had ever eaten, accompanied by an abundance of red wine which Golo drank, not so much from fear but out of politeness.

After dinner Golo requested to take leave again, but Jamshid asked him to wait. He sat on the sofa, feeling lightheaded from the effect of alcohol.

"So do you know how to prepare a *manqal* for the opium?" Jamshid asked.

"Oh no, sorry Sir. I have never done it in my life," Golo responded apologetically for his obvious ignorance of a very important matter.

Jamshid laughed: "I don't understand these Afghans. They deal with opium, but don't smoke it. Okay then, you stay here and continue with your wine."

Golo was extremely drunk. Greed and nervousness forced him to drink excessively; it had been a long time since he had last touched alcohol. He was a poor man now and could not afford alcohol, but when it was offered, he could not stop himself from drinking, especially if his boss encouraged him. Golo was so drunk by the time Jamshid returned and sat next to him that he could not have moved even if he had tried.

Before knowing what was happening, he felt Jamshid's hand caressing his thighs and reaching the zipper of his trouser. Golo had never experienced a homosexual encounter before and never thought about it in detail. In the presence of a powerful boss and effected by alcohol, he was not in a position to resist. In fact, when Jamshid started to touch his member, to his surprise, he became instantly erect. Advancing to this stage was part of a great game for Jamshid. He was simply thinking of Golo as another product that he had purchased that he found to be handsome, and therefore, worth retaining for longer use to satisfy his desire. That night, while Golo floated between the earth and sky, he was encouraged to enter Jamshid, by the boss himself.

The following day Jamshid acted as if nothing had happened between them. Golo was the driver and Mr. Jamshid his boss. Nothing appeared to have changed apart from a massive rise in Golo's salary. Golo would be safe and could keep his job as long as he kept secrets. He knew that. Their sexual encounters also continued. Golo was not a homosexual, but an opportunist. He knew that many Afghan men and women were forced to serve their masters one way or another. He also realised that the biggest secret he had to keep was not Mr. Jamshid's habit of smoking opium, but their homosexual relationship.

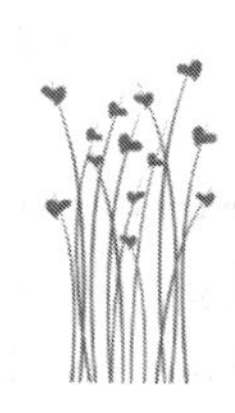

CHAPTER 31

The month of April was beautiful. The parks of Tehran blossomed with flowers. The land was covered with lush green grass, trees full of leaves and birds chirping happy songs. Jamshid, as usual, sat at the back of the car, reading his newspaper as he listened to western classical music. He was so absorbed that he did not notice the car slow down. He only became aware of the situation when he heard a sudden banging against his car window. He ordered Golo to turn down the volume. The road leading to the factory was blocked by protesters shouting: "Death to the Shah, death to his family and death to his government."

Jamshid felt a rush of panic: "Lock the doors! Why didn't you tell me what was happening?" he said with fear and anger in his voice.

"Sir, they suddenly appeared out of nowhere," Golo replied.

There was no time for further conversation. Demonstrators grew larger and bolder in numbers as they slammed the car with their fists. Golo was young and did not panic, but noticed that the colour of Jamshid's face was white with fear. This was a matter of life and death, he thought. Recently protesters had attacked government officials and rich people, injuring them. They must have known that Jamshid was the son of a prominent minister and a wealthy man. Suddenly, from nowhere a brick was thrown at the window. It shattered the side window into pieces, but without causing any injury. Jamshid commanded: "Golo, they are mad! Do something!" But the road was blocked and Golo could not find a gap between the demonstrators. Another person attacked the car, this time with an iron bar. Jamshid jumped with fear, screaming "They will surely kill us."

It was at this point that Golo took a decision; he put his foot down hard on the accelerator, creating considerable noise from the engine and steered left to a small road leading to a residential area. The noise and speed took the demonstrators by surprise and they had no choice but give way to the car. They only started to run after it when the car entered the smaller road. Golo was a confident driver. He drove fast without panicking and did not slow down until they had lost all the demonstrators pursuing them.

Eventually, Golo slowed down and checked his mirror to see if his boss was all right. Jamshid met his gaze in the mirror, now composed, but ashamed of his earlier panic.

"Well done," Jamshid said.

Golo smiled with satisfaction and asked, "Where to, Sir?"

It was only at that moment that Jamshid realised that he could not proceed to his factory and after some quick thinking ordered Golo to drive to the country villa instead.

In the villa, Jamshid indulged himself, immersed in the pleasure of flesh while Golo, a loyal servant, responded to his master. Their intimacy released Jamshid's tension, at least momentarily. Jamshid almost loved Golo. The reason that he could not love him completely was because he was paying for Golo's services. He knew that from Golo's point of view he was merely a service provider, no more. Jamshid could not complain about his life. He had never liked the factory anyway. He was an artist and disliked being called a factory owner. Rather an artist with a handsome man on his side. When he got news that the factory would remain closed, he did not mind. Not at all.

It was Jamshid's habit to read various newspapers on a daily basis. They informed him of what was happening; he was therefore not completely ignorant of Iran's turmoil. The country raged by the anger of demonstrators, shouting death threats to the Shah. He blamed his father, not the anger of the demonstrators, for his own misfortune. His father had made him return to Iran, to his home country. He thought there was no future for him in a country that was not interested in his art, as well as not accepting his personal life. As a gay artist he had no future in Iran. In contrast, he had been very happy in Paris, among artists and lovers. Now he had to accept an uneducated Afghan as his lover. Sex and opium was a form of escape from this misery. He had no regard for his father, but without his money and support he could not exist either.

Some days later, when Jamshid was trying hard to forget about Iran and its problems, the telephone rang. His father urged him to come to Tehran. Jamshid assumed, as usual, that his father would give him a lecture on how to look after the factory and their properties. But he was surprised to learn that his father had been removed from his job. Sacking his father had been a calculated political manoeuvre to calm down the protesters. The Shah found it necessary to bow to some of the many demands in an attempt of reducing his family's political influence. Jamshid was informed that he must go back to France accompanied by his mother. His father would remain in Iran to show his loyalty and support to the Shah. This bad news for his father turned out to be excellent news for Jamshid.

It was only at the last minute, before leaving the country, that he summoned Golo to his study and rewarded him for his service. He received two thousand dollars. The following day Jamshid was on the plane and Golo was left behind, jobless. The amount of money seemed enormous for Golo, but was nothing for Jamshid, who was always generous with his lovers.

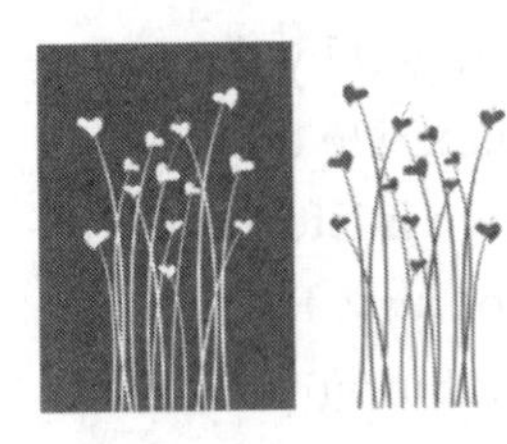

CHAPTER 32

Hamid had developed a fondness for the bitter taste of Russian vodka. It was always available for him, free of cost. He never asked where it came from. It was always provided by someone and most of the time it was from his friend, the doctor. They met frequently. After the success of the revolution, Nasrat and Hamid became even closer friends. The doctor liked literature and Hamid's knowledge of it was fully appreciated.

They sat in the doctor's garden one warm night in August. Hamid listened to the sound of peace and war while drinking vodka. There was peace in the beautiful house, but war outside. The radio played the sitar, by one of the greatest Indian musicians, Ustad Rais Khan, well known in Afghanistan. The fragrance of jasmine trees filled the garden. Hamid's eyes were closed while he listened to the music. Nasrat sat next to him.

Without opening his eyes Hamid said, "You know Nasrat, there is a similar flower in India which drives young men and women crazy. Its fragrance spreads at night and they call it *raat ki rani,* the queen of the night."

"What a wonderful name," the doctor said.

They continued to listen to the music of peace. Slowly Hamid opened his eyes but did not look at the doctor; instead he gazed towards the clear sky. There was a full moon. To Hamid it seemed as if the moon hosted all the shiny stars.

With the arrival of the night
my lover came
I shut the door to be alone with my lover
and did not open it even for the moon to enter.

"Wah! Wonderful Comrade. So appropriate for the occasion. Whose poem is it?" the doctor asked.

"I don't remember but I love it," Hamid replied.

"Read it again."

With the arrival of the night
my lover...

Suddenly, the sound of continuous gunshot, not far from Nasrat's house tore the heart of silent Kabul. Hamid jumped from his seat.

"Don't panic, Comrade," the doctor said. Hamid was embarrassed.

"We are in safe hands. Our streets are guarded by soldiers of a country, which has the best armed forces in the world, The Soviet Union," Nasrat said.

"I am not scared. I was absorbed by the music and taken by surprise by the loud noise," Hamid explained.

"In that case I will take you somewhere to get used to such noise," the doctor said, while laughing. "After that you will be prepared, Comrade Hamid."

"What do you have in mind exactly?" asked Hamid. "I hope you will not surprise me again."

"No surprise this time Hamid," the doctor said. "I want you to read your poetry for our comrades who are fighting the enemy. I want you to be the Mayakovsky of our nation. Ignite fire in the heart of our comrades. Make them go forward to crash our enemy. Do you understand?" Without waiting to hear his answer, Nasrat continued, "Write poems, Comrade. Now you don't have to worry about our enemies. No one will stop you from supporting the revolution."

"It's from Yazdi," shouted Hamid.

"What?" Nasrat said, taken by surprise by Hamid's sudden change of tone.

"I remember now. The poem that I was reciting before the shooting started, is from Yazdi, another revolutionary poet," Hamid said. They both laughed.

Outside on the street, only the Russian soldier, who guarded the nearby road, knew the reason behind the shooting. He almost finished the magazine of his kalashnikov. He had seen a shadow that belonged to a stray dog and shot in that direction. Was he drunk? Perhaps not. There was a substance easily available among the Russian soldiers: known as Afghan black or hashish. The Russians loved the Afghan black, while the Afghan comrades discovered their love for Russian vodka. No one knew if the Russian soldier had been under the influence of hashish or he was simply scared by the shadow, as if it were the shadow of an enemy. The road was completely empty since curfew. Before being posted in Kabul, the same soldier had served on the border to Pakistan and had become jumpy since then. This country was a real war zone; only Kabulis, including Hamid, did not know about it. But high ranking officials from the Afghan People's Party and the Russians knew what was really happening. Rural Afghanistan was not safe and Russians, even with all their power, could not control rural Afghanistan.

Later that night, Hamid sat in the backseat of his car driven by his driver. The streets were deserted. Kabul was enveloped in absolute silence. The only person he saw on the road was a Russian soldier at a check point. Hamid knew the code for the night. There would be no problem if his car was stopped. He enjoyed the quietness and felt reassured by the presence of Russian soldiers standing next to their tanks. A smile appeared on his face. Before the revolution he couldn't have guessed that one day he would smile to himself. He smiled thinking that his enemy – the animal – was under a pile of dirt. Hamid knew that many people like the animal were against the revolution and he was ready to defend the revolution from them. He could do all this, but could not write a poem when someone else chose the subject. Lying in bed he thought of composing a poem but nothing happened. It was almost morning when he found the solution. He would go to see his comrades in the provinces with Mayakovsky.

The following morning Hamid was back in the old library in the centre of the town, looking for Mayakovsky's poems. He wanted to copy and read them, while he was visiting the comrades. The revolution had a solution for everything.

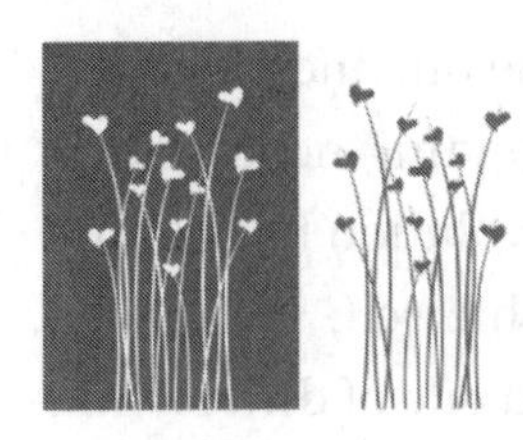

CHAPTER 33

Kabul was beautiful in September. The hot summer was replaced by the beginning of autumn. Trees were decorated with gold and green colours. The parks of Kabul had dedicated gardeners that knew how to make them attractive with exotic flowers and green grass. Afghans loved the parks and visited them during the day, since there was a curfew at night. From the time that the communist government had taken over, there was freedom for the youth. One could easily spot young couples sitting under the trees chatting with each other – talking about love and life. There were no restrictions by the government. In fact, the new leaders were seen as progressive and encouraged young men and women to meet and enjoy life.

September was also the time when the famous melon *kharbooza* from Balkh filled the market. The fruit was so delicious that historians and kings that had lived in Kabul mentioned it in their memoirs. Early morning there was a knock on the door. Nasrat had come to take Hamid for a drive to the rural area.

"We are going towards Balkh," Nasrat informed when he picked up Hamid from his apartment.

"Oh excellent. I like the scenic road towards Balkh, but I don't understand why you keep the name of the destination a secret."

"I don't want to spoil the surprise. But have you been to Balkh?"

"Many times."

"*Kharbooza* tastes different there."

"Yeah. People who bring *kharbooza* here, pick them raw."

"That must be the reason that they are not sweet in Kabul."

"When our revolution gets rid of reactionary forces, we will go together to Balkh and it won't be like this."

"What do you have in mind?"

"We will travel alone in a private car without drivers. We can pause in Salang to watch the river and drink vodka. And then again in Tashkurgan."

He was referring to an amazing landscape in Tashkurgan, a unique spot where the mountain cliff was steep. Legend had it that in this very spot, Ali, the cousin of Prophet Mohammed, came and sliced the mountain with his sword in two pieces, carving a narrow path where today a river flows adjacent to a picturesque road.

Hamid found himself seated next to the doctor on the road to Balkh, but Balkh was not their destination. Forty kilometres after Kabul they would take a road to a place well known for its natural beauty: Panjshir. Finally, Nasrat revealed the name of their destination. Sitting in the armoured Russian vehicle, Hamid remembered a famous song about Panjshir:

Let's go to Sangeraan
many beautiful women live there
women, amongst flowers and nightingales
women who appreciate your love

They were in a convoy of armoured vehicle and tanks. Hamid almost suffocated inside. He had always wanted to see the beauty of nature along this road. Friends, who had gone there in the past, told him about the beauty.

"The road goes along the mountain on one side and on the other is a wild river. You can hear the sound of the river while you are travelling. You must stop to have lunch in one of the restaurants along the road and listen to the sound of the river."

In the armoured vehicle the tiny windows were not used to look at the scenery, but for the soldiers to check if the enemy was close. Panjshir changed from being one of the most beautiful places in Afghanistan to one of the most dangerous. It was the heart of resistance between the Soviet Union and the Afghan government. After a long time it seemed that the enemy has been crashed. The leader of the resistance fighters had been defeated and had gone to the top of the mountains, but were followed by the Russians in their helicopters. The government was determined to find him. A person like Hamid was encouraged to go to Panjshir and to see for himself that no one could resist the mighty force of the Soviet Union. But Hamid could not see from the darkness of the vehicle that victory also come with many sacrifices. The entire road was littered with destroyed tanks and armoured vehicles. The enemy was not as weak as the government had propagated. Despite all this it was a time for celebration. The enemy had left and there was peace in Panjshir.

They reached Panjshir when it was dark and spent the night in the army compound drinking vodka with the political agent of the army, a very serious follower of Lenin. They talked about life in Panjshir as well as politics. The agent assured them that no one could stop the flow of communism from reaching neighbouring countries. No place would be left. There would be only one country and that would be the kingdom of communism. Such convictions reminded Hamid that some mullahs also believed that in the end there would be only one kingdom and that would be the kingdom of Islam.

It was quiet outside. There was no sound of gunshots. The enemy had escaped. After drinking plenty of vodka, later that night, Hamid fell asleep in a room shared by the doctor and the political agent. It was a peaceful sleep and in his dream, Hamid saw himself fishing in the beautiful river. When he got up, he could not understand the meaning of the dream. He never thought of fishing before and didn't know how to. He thought one must have the skill to fish.

When he told his dream to Nasrat in the morning, he said, "Well Comrade, it is never too late to learn to fish. Maybe we can go fishing in the river that sings songs of communism this afternoon." They both laughed.

About 10 am, after they finished their breakfast, the doctor informed Hamid, that there would be a gathering in the centre of the town to celebrate the victory of the government. They left the army compound with some officers and soldiers and walked towards the town centre. Hamid found the place remarkably peaceful. At the gathering there were cheers and speeches. Hamid was also called to step up to the mike to read his poem. He walked up to the platform and reached into his pocket to retrieve the poem of Mayakovski:

My esteemed Comrades of future world!
Searching among these days' petrified nonsense,
traversing the horizon of our times,
you, maybe,
will investigate about me as well.
And, maybe, your learned men will admit,
with their polished overpowering a swarm of problems,
once upon a time lived a man of boiled water
who was practicing enemy of raw water.

When he was finished, a few minutes later, among the cheering and clapping, he suddenly felt great pain, as if a knife had pierced his chest. He just managed to see that his white shirt was covered with blood before he collapsed. Someone had shot him.

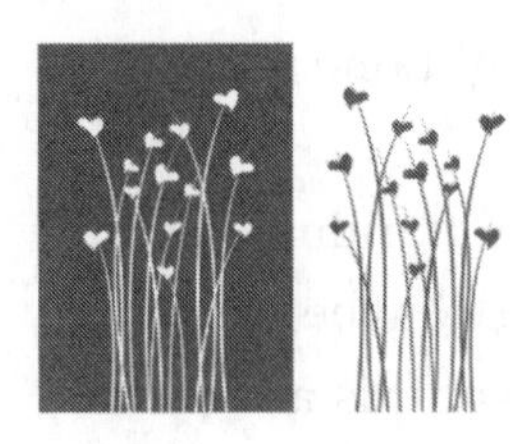

CHAPTER 34

Hamid had been lying in a hospital bed fighting for his life for more than two weeks. The bullet had entered his chest and came out on the other side without exploding inside his body, just missing the important organs. This was the reason that he was still alive. He was fortunate enough to have the best Russian doctors look after him. After he was shot he was flown back to the capital by helicopter and left in the best hospital, managed by Russian doctors. No one could find out who shot Hamid, but everyone knew that he was a resistance fighter that knew his country well – well enough to aim, to shoot and to disappear. Panjshir was not so safe after all.

The doctors were greatly optimistic about Hamid's chance of survival. Sixteen days later Hamid woke from his coma and saw his mother by his side weeping.

"Son, how are you?" his mother asked.

"Mother, where am I?" he asked.

"You are in the hospital, my sweet son. You have been here for a long time," she replied. "How could I live without my children? And why did you go to Panjshir?" she asked. At that moment the doctor came in. He told her that the patient needed to rest.

From then on there were continuous visits. Rahmat, his father, mother and Nasrat came to the hospital every day and each night a member of the family stayed next to Hamid's bed. The other person who regularly came to see Hamid was Safa.

Four days before leaving the hospital, Safa was visiting Hamid. She had come with a book of poetry that she bought to keep his mind away from hospital boredom. Hamid looked at the book and smiled.

"Another book? I have not yet finished the previous one you brought for me some days ago," Hamid said.

"Then read fast because I will bring you another one soon," Safa replied with a smile. Hamid went through the pages and read some stanzas out loud.

She travels in my voice
page by page
she fills me
I become a book of poetry
description, reflection
a mirror, a book
a voice which echoes
sadness, happiness, love, distrust
in one melody.

She travels in my voice
I become songs
songs of deep sorrows, wide ecstasy
song of wind
reaching the shores of harmony.

She travels in my voice
I become whisper
whispering stories
to flowers, to moon
to each grain of sand, in Sahara.

"You read with so much passion and your voice is made for reading poetry. I am sure the guy who shot you was jealous of your talent," Safa said with laughter.

Suddenly, not following the same line of conversation, Hamid said: "Safa, I am in love with you." Hamid was searching for the right words, "I have been in love with you ever since I saw you, but I did not have the courage…"

"Oh no, please stop. I don't want to hear this," Safa shouted.

"But why? Is there someone else?" Hamid asked with a pleading voice. Before he could hear her answer she had left the room, fighting back her tears. She did not return to the hospital again.

Hamid became depressed. Just before going to Panjshir he had been so optimistic about life and now he was in the hospital with a broken heart. When Nasrat came to see him he told him that he was deeply depressed. Soon the doctor found out the reason and felt sorry for him.

For Safa, love had lost its meaning. She had been so deeply in love with Golo that she had disregarded all rules of society. She had believed in him and had planned to be with him for the rest of her life. That was the main reason that she had allowed herself to be so open with Golo and yet he had gone. She still wanted to convince herself that he would return back to Afghanistan and she thought about him quite often. But sometimes she wished that she had never met Golo. She also thought about Hamid, a wonderful and highly educated man, committed to his cause of helping his people – just like her. But now being with Hamid was impossible in a simple friendship. Now that Hamid had declared his love for her she couldn't sleep anymore and thought about her future at night. Where could she go from here? She wanted to stay away from men, but Afghan society did not allow women to live alone, especially if the woman was beautiful. She was beautiful and many men came to her house asking her father for her hand in marriage. But she always refused saying that it was not yet time. Her father was a modern and kind man and did not allow himself to make a decision for his daughter. She knew that one day her family would remind her that the time for marriage had come.

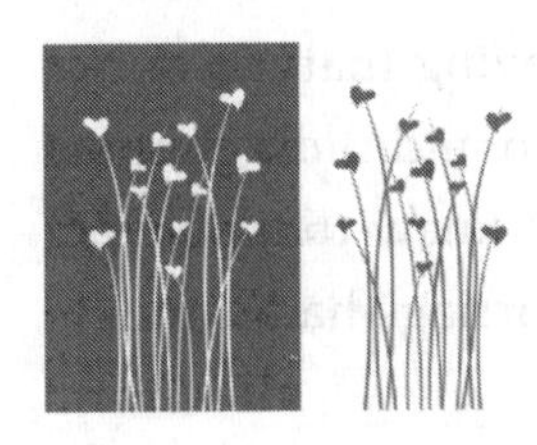

CHAPTER 35

A letter from Roshan arrived after a long time. In fact that was only her second letter since she had left for Germany.

My dear sister Safa jan salam,
I'm sorry for not writing in so long. Please don't think that I do not want to be in touch. The reason that I couldn't write is because I have been sick. Life is not easy for a woman from Afghanistan here in Germany, especially when there is little support from her husband. Kamran, my husband, has been difficult. He is not such a traditional person and often complains that I don't know enough about the western way of living, I am too slow in learning the language and top of that not so good in bed. Kamran wants an experienced virgin. But how a virgin can be experienced? He has told me about his ex-girlfriend and how good she was. The only reason that he could not marry her was because she had boyfriends before him. One day the sky collapsed on my head when I saw him with another woman, hand in hand. I had gone shopping and Kamran thought I would not see them.

After that I lost my appetite and began losing weight. Kamran took me to the doctor. He told him that I was depressed and it would be better for both of us if I went back to Afghanistan to visit my family because my depression was probably related to homesickness. I never told Kamran what really bothered me. The good news is that I will be in Kabul soon and would love to meet you again, my dearest friend. You are closer to me than my family.

By the way I hear terrible stories about our country. Russian soldiers forcing people from rural areas to take refuge in Pakistan and Iran. There are

now 2 million refugees in Iran and 3 million in Pakistan. The Mujahidin in Pakistan are not kind. Some months ago a distant relative of mine came to Germany as an asylum seeker. Her husband, an educated man, was killed by one of the leaders of the Mujahidin in Peshawar. This man wanted to marry my distant relative, but she and her family preferred the educated man and let them marry. The leader of the Mujahidin did not forget this and held a grudge against my distant relative and her husband. He made a political case against the husband saying that he was a communist spy watching the Mujahidin. He was captured not long ago in Peshawar and killed. She says that there are many private prisons owned by the Mujahidin in Pakistan and that the government ignores this. How awful! Escaping Afghanistan from the Russians only to be killed by a Mujahidin in Pakistan. May Allah save our country.
Your sister,
Roshan

The letter couldn't have come at a better time. It made Safa happy and she read it many times. The thought of meeting Roshan again robbed Safa from her sleep. She was extremely excited. How wonderful it would be to see her again and talk about their life, the innocent life that they shared without men and their troubles.

Safa was avoiding Hamid because she did not want to see the pain in his eyes. His love for her was painful and she cared enough for him not to cause him any more pain. She thought if she kept away from him, maybe one day he would forget about her and they could become friends again.

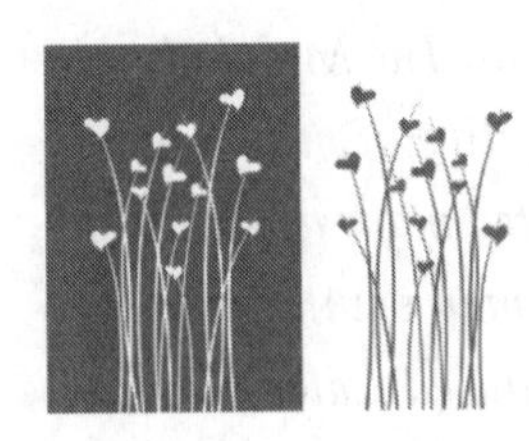

CHAPTER 36

A month later Roshan arrived in Kabul and the first person that she wanted to meet was her friend Safa. Safa went to see her in her parents' house and was shocked to see Roshan so thin and pale. What had happened to her? She wanted to ask, but stopped herself thinking that if she showed signs of worry it would make Roshan to feel even worse.

"Oh, Safa jan, how nice of you to come. I missed you so much! How is kahala Nasrin and how is my uncle?"

Safa sat on a comfortable *toshak* next to Roshan, drinking tea and eating chocolate that she had brought from Germany. Nasrin had left them alone in the room. The two girls needed to catch up and talk about their lives since Roshan had left Kabul.

"Open your present," Roshan said, pointing to the package.

"Roshan jan, the best present is seeing you. I missed you so much!"

Safa kissed Roshan's cheeks with emotion once more. They had been crying with happiness and were speechless for a long time.

"Come on, open it. I chose it myself going from shop to shop, even though I did not have much energy."

Safa opened the package. It was a fashionable blue blouse.

"Do you like it? Try it on. It will go well with a pair of jeans."

"Oh, I love it. It's great," Safa said. She took off her own blouse and tried on the new one.

"It's perfect. How did you remember my size?"

"I remembered the hamam. I saw your naked body there, remember?"

"Ha hamammmmm…"

"I wish we had never gone there. If I hadn't gone there, I would have never ended up in Germany."

"Please don't be so pessimistic. I am sure that Kamran will change. He must have been shocked by what happened to you and he must care. That is why you are here. You must tell him what has caused you to become like this."

"Yes, I will. I thought about it and the best way to stop suffering is to tell him exactly what is bothering me. He is my doctor, because he has the real cure. He has to accept me and give up his girlfriend."

"Yes, you silly, that is the best way. You have your own answers."

"Yes I do, but do you have your own answers?"

"What do you mean?"

"I mean what is the reason for not accepting Hamid's love? I know him very well. He was friend of Golo's. He is a wonderful person."

"It is not easy Roshan jan," Safa said and began sobbing.

"Why is it not easy?" Roshan asked in surprise. "Are you engaged to someone else?"

"No, that is not the case. You said it in your own letter. Afghan men have double standards. They all want virgins."

"I don't understand. What are you talking about?"

"Well, okay. I am not virgin anymore. No one as good as Hamid would marry me now. The best chance I have is marrying someone who already has a wife. Even then I will be treated like a servant without honour."

"You are killing me. Please explain what exactly happened."

"It was Golo who took my virginity away."

"What? Golo, my brother?"

"Yes."

"Did he rape you?"

"No, he promised to marry me. I became his lover. I have always loved your family and wanted to become your real sister. I wanted to be part of your family."

"You fool. That idiot Golo had lots of contacts with different girls."

"I didn't know Roshan. I didn't know." Safa started crying.

"There must be a solution for this."

"If you are thinking of Golo marrying me, you are wrong. He disappeared and to be honest I am not even sure if I still want to marry him. He broke my heart."

"In that case I must talk to Hamid."

"Please don't. To Hamid I am pure. That is the image in his mind. I want that image to stay the same."

"You are wrong. That is not your real image. Your real image is what you are. Still pure, but you are hiding behind a false image."

"It is the image of a battered woman with a broken heart."

"Love can repair broken hearts. Hamid loves you and I am going to talk to him."

"Oh, please Roshan, don't torture me."

"We are in the middle of a revolution. Getting married and having children before the revolution took away your life."

"I had an abortion. The doctor said that I might never get pregnant again."

When Safa told her this, Roshan burst into tears. She realized that her friends' suffering was far bigger than her own.

CHAPTER 37

Safa's story made Roshan very sad. She genuinely liked both Hamid and Safa and now found herself in a difficult position. She felt sorry for both of them. Roshan suggested something that surprised Safa. She said that she should look at her future and forget her sorrows. She also mentioned that Hamid was a modern and educated man who was a serious follower of modern thinking. Maybe Hamid would be able to forget what happened to her. Hamid knew Afghan society and its hypocrisy. After all he was almost raped himself. She suggested that Safa should think about it positively and allow Hamid to be her future husband. She advised her not to tell her story to Hamid, that it was not necessary. But Safa refused.

That night Roshan could not sleep even with the sleeping pills that the doctor had given her. After a week she finally decided to meet Hamid. She was in a dilemma, but wanted to see Hamid anyway. If Roshan revealed to Hamid the reason why Safa was not seeing him there could be two results: Hamid could decide to forget Safa or he could understand the way the society was or even better forgive Safa's mistake. In this age of revolution not many people stayed pure. Women were raped by revolutionaries and the Mujahidin alike. Who was Hamid to judge? Hamid did not seem judgmental to her anyway. So she decided to go for it; it was worth the try. Roshan decided not to tell Safa what she was about to do.

Hamid was now completely healthy and back in his office when Roshan went to see him. She was surprised to find him in a big office, behind a huge desk with his head buried in files and paper.

She knew him since he was a child. She used to go to their house and meet him with his brother Rahmat. Hamid also came to their house very often because he was Golo's best friend. However, she saw less and less of Hamid and more of the rest of the family. Whenever people asked where he was, the mother replied that Hamid was in the library. He had developed the nickname: the boy who lived in the library. Hamid did not notice that someone had entered the office and continued to read until Roshan spoke:

"Sir, I have come to lodge a complaint." Hamid was a bit shocked and looked in the direction of the voice. "What kind of complaint, madam?"

"You didn't come to my wedding."

"Oh, I see. Do you work for our ministry?" he said with laughter. "I'm sorry, these days there are too many weddings and I have so much work."

"Do you only go to the weddings of your colleagues?"

"Oh no. Sometimes I go to friends' and relatives' weddings as well. But I don't think that you are a relative of mine."

"How about friends?"

"Madam, these days my sense of humour does not exist and I am afraid yours is wasted on me."

"Shame on you Hamid, that you don't recognize me."

The office was dark and the curtains were drawn. Hamid focused his gaze and recognized the woman in surprise. "Oh my god, it is you Roshan! But you have changed."

"Of course, we all change and it's been a long time."

"You are right. I couldn't come to the wedding but I always ask about you when I see your father and Nasrin on the streets or when they came to our house. They told me that you were very happy in Germany."

"Did they?"

"Oh, yes."

"And are you happy, Hamid?

"Please sit and we can talk. Sit on the sofa and I will come and sit next to you. Tell me, when did you come back to Kabul?"

Hamid ordered tea. When it arrived Roshan asked the same question again.

"I asked if you were happy, Hamid."

"What kind of a question is that? I am not married."

"But the person whom you want to marry is my friend: Safa. If you had come to our house only once you would have met her. She still lives in my parents' house," Roshan said with a hint of sarcasm in her voice.

"I am dumbfounded. Is she the same person? My mother talked about your neighbour after she visited your house."

"You are so busy writing poetry and making plots for your characters that you do not see real characters, Hamid jan."

"How do you know that I love Safa?"

"She told me."

"And did she tell you that she refused me?"

"Yes, but she has a reason for that."

"What reason?"

"She believes that she doesn't deserve your love."

"What kind of nonsense is that?"

"She is not what you think she is."

"What kind of explanation is that?"

"She was engaged before to my brother Golo."

"What kind of engagement? Golo is my friend too. I would have known."

"Well, it was secret, an agreement between Golo and Safa. Safa requested that it be kept secret until she finished her studies. Unfortunately Golo was not reliable and disappeared."

"Oh, dear me. It seems like an amazing episode of an exciting drama."

"No need to be sarcastic Hamid. You are too nice for that."

"So what do you want me to do?"

"She loves you."

"How can she love me if she is engaged to your brother?"

"Not anymore. Golo broke their engagement. He disappeared but is planning to come back, not to get married to Safa. He is just coming to see me."

"Oh! I have a headache."

"She loves you and will accept your love, provided that you forget her engagement with Golo."

"How can I forget?"

"Hamid jan, I have come here to ask for the forgiveness of two people that I love. First forgive Safa for her mistake. In a way she was cheated. Then forgive Golo, whom I care less about, but he is nevertheless my brother. If you decide to take revenge and clean up the dishonour that Golo has caused you, it is your choice. You are the man of power and he will be here within two weeks. I love him, but I also understand our society. The reason that I ask you to forgive him is because you are not a hypocrite like the rest of our society. You are not like my husband. I went as a virgin to Germany and look at what he has done to me. He says I am a virgin, but not experienced enough in love."

"I have to think about it."

"Think about it, but not for too long. Safa will not remain single. She has a chance to get married not to a perfect person, but she will nevertheless. That person will rob you of your happiness not Golo. Golo would happily leave Safa to you. He is not man enough."

"You know the reason that I bury myself in these papers? It's to forget my sorrows."

"We all create our sorrows, Hamid. First you created them when you thought that Safa did not love you. Now you have created them because she loves you and yet in your eyes she is not pure anymore. Think about it when I am gone. Think about it without burying yourself in papers. Face the problem and don't run away from it. God bless you. I must go now."

What a life, Hamid thought. He must have been born to live with sorrows. How silly he was thinking that love would replace all the sadness with happiness and cure his wounded heart. Love for him was purity and yet he could not find purity around him. How wrong he had been thinking that Safa was a decent and innocent girl. That image was now torn. Anger and hate filled his heart.

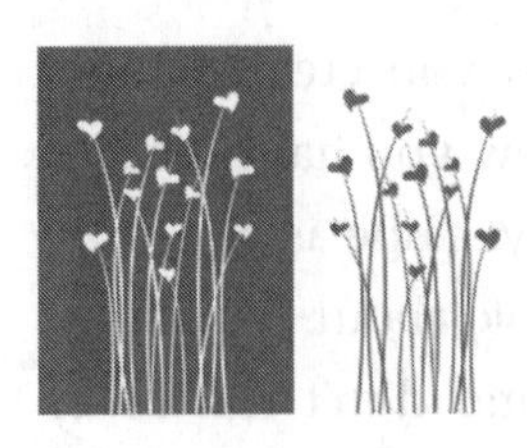

CHAPTER 38

Hamid engaged a police to inform him when Golo came back from Iran. There was so much anger in his heart. Yet he decided to let Golo meet his family first as a mark of respect for Roshan and his friendship with Golo. But the day arrived when Golo was brought to Hamid's office as if he was a criminal. There was no sign of friendship on Hamid's face. Golo was not aware of what was happening and was about to shake hands with Hamid, but he refused. Now Golo realised that something was amiss and trembled with fear. Maybe someone had reported him as an anti-revolutionist!

All he managed to say was: "What is the problem Hamid jan? Have I done something wrong? I am not against the government."

"I wish I didn't know you, you little shit."

"What have I done, for God's sake?"

"You little spoiled ass, you never know what you have done."

"Please Hamid, tell me."

"I never imagined that you shit would do something to me."

"What?"

"You robbed me of my happiness. You thought that only you deserved happiness and the whole universe was there to serve you."

"But what have I done?"

"I could kill you for what you have done to Safa."

"What do you mean? And why are you talking about Safa?"

"I am in love or was in love with her until I was informed that you damaged her."

"But how could I know that you would fall in love with her one day?"

"Stop it, you idiot."

Hamid threw a book at Golo but it missed him. He jumped out of his chair to go and hit him but stopped midway. Silence continued between them until Golo began to explain.

"I'm really sorry, Hamid."

"Sorry is not enough Golo. The time has come for you to be punished. Otherwise you will go on robbing other people's honour. You are a thief and a dangerous one at that."

"Please, Hamid. I am not the same person anymore. I suffered so much in Iran."

"I don't care."

"I was in a country where there was no honour for people like me. They did what they wanted to do with Afghan refugees. You are the man who wants to defend victims. I am one of those victims now."

"Enough, you charlatan."

Hamid asked for the police and did not listen to Golo who was begging to save his life. The police took him away.

After Golo left, Hamid fixed his eyes on the wall in front of him. Life became a film screen and in it he saw his childhood with Golo. Memories came back of the time when Golo was his only friend and they went to parks and the countryside together, to see the beauty of nature. How life had changed and now his friend had become his enemy. Life was so unpredictable. He was deep in thought and did not notice Nasrat enter his office.

"Perfect timing Comrade, perfect timing. I need a cigarette."

"What? You have never smoked before."

"Only when I am celebrating."

"And what is the reason for the celebration?"

"I killed my enemy."

"Enemy of the revolution you mean, Comrade."

"Comrade, I am the revolution."

Nasrat was shocked. He did not imagine that Hamid could perceive the revolution this way. Of course, what Hamid said was a quotation from Lenin, but Hamid was not Lenin.

Nasrat was wrong. Hamid did not kill anyone. What he meant was that he had killed hate and revenge in his heart. He did not send Golo to prison or to his death. The only thing he did was to send Golo to serve the army and to defend the revolution against the enemy. That is what he had been doing and it would be the same for Rahmat. When Rahmat was old enough to join the army, Hamid would send him there. He thought about taking revenge on Golo for a long time and had the option to kill him. But then he remembered something that his father had said: the pleasure of forgiveness is greater than the pleasure of taking revenge. He decided to break the cycle of revenge in a society that was well known for such actions. Even if Golo had slept with Safa, how could he have known that one day Hamid would love her?

When he finally managed to forgive Golo, he easily found love in his heart again and forgot what had happened between Safa and Golo. Safa was just as pure and innocent as a child. She was a victim herself and must have suffered a great deal. She did not deserve to suffer anymore. Hamid thought that the time had come to heal the wounds that were killing Safa's heart and replace them with love, instead of fear and uncertainty.

Forgiveness brought love back to Hamid's heart. Now alone in his office, with no one to disturb him, he opened the poetry book of his favourite poet Nizami and read aloud as if reading to an audience:

O lovers, lovers it is time
to set out from the world.
I hear a drum in my soul's ear
coming from the depths of the stars.

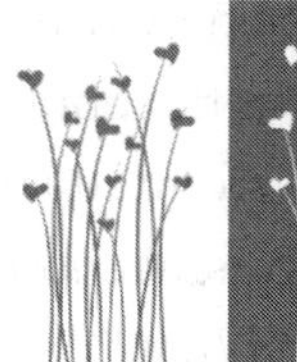

CHAPTER 39

It was way beyond regular office hours. Hamid was busy putting finishing touches to his newspaper. The Truth, Sergey Aleynikov his Russian *moshawer,* consultant was helping him. After they had finished their editorial work, the paper would go to print. Workers required for the printing process were held back at the publishing house for yet another night.

"Another vodka, Comrade Hamid?"

"I suppose this is the only way to keep going, but it is hard for them."

"For who?"

"For these workers. Do you think it is a good idea to at least pay them overtime?"

"And where is the extra pay to come from?"

"I thought your kind government could, as the protector of proletariat. Your government has been supporting us in our projects since the revolution."

"Comrade Soviet Union is in deep crises. The war has cost too much. We are not fighting illiterate Mujahidin. We are fighting the Chinese, the Americans, the Arabs, Pakistanis, Iranians and the list is endless. Comrade, when our people tried to successfully support the October revolution, no one helped us. It was the people of the Soviet Union who printed papers, dug the canals for irrigation, and worked in the agricultural farms nonstop. All voluntarily, Comrade!"

"I suppose the answer to that argument is another Russian vodka."

"Yes Comrade. That will be provided."

Sergey was filling Hamid's glass when the phone rang. Hamid picked up the phone.

"Comrade the blood suckers are spreading poisonous words," Doctor Nasrat shouted from the other side of the line.

"What?"

"Hamid do you read foreign newspapers?"

"Of course, Comrade. It is part of my responsibility."

"So what do you think about it?"

"Can you be a bit more specific?"

"Did you read the article in The Times?"

"Are you referring to the article about our land reforms?"

"Exactly, they say that our land reforms have failed."

"Well, they argue that when the land was taken from the big landlords and given to the farmers, our government did not protect the farmers. The farmers never managed to have access to these lands awarded to them, because the landlords have their own private army and don't allow anyone to touch their land."

"Yes they claim we do not posses enough power in the rural areas and on top of that the mullahs argue that this kind of reform is anti-Islamic."

"So what shall I do Comrade?"

"Write an article in counter-attack and publish it in Kabul Times, our English newspaper."

"English newspaper?"

"Yes. Those idiots must read it in their own language and become aware that we know what they are up to."

"In English?"

"Yes in English and your English is good enough, no?"

"Well yes, it is good enough."

"Don't worry about the language. Sergey will help you with that, but you must write a response. Read their article again."

Doctor Nasrat put the receiver down without saying goodbye, a sign that he was under pressure. Hamid stared at his glass of vodka and gulped the contents of the glass.

"Another one, Comrade. It appears that we will spend the entire night here and no worker is to go home."

"Quite, that is the spirit Comrade."

"We must postpone the publication of the article 'Women's right after Revolution in Afghanistan' and replace it with the story of the 'Success of the Land Reform.' "

"Okay, good idea."

"I will write it now and you may correct it, if there are any mistakes."

"*Nazdrovia* Comrade," Sergey picked up his glass.

"*Ba salamat,*" Hamid gulped another glass of vodka and started writing about the land reforms. The following morning when doctor Nasrat left his bed and came to his breakfast table he read in the *Kabul Times*:

To whom does the land belong? I ask you my dear countrymen. Does it belong to those who do no labour in the fields, resting in their posh houses, indulging in delicious drinks and food or, to those who labour under the hot sun every day, to produce wealth for the lazy people who call themselves landowners? I am sure most of you, apart from the landlords and some ignorant religious leaders, would agree that the farmers should be the just owners. Since you are the majority, our Government who kept their word to protect the proletariat and the farmers decided to carry out the land reforms. As a result, the poor farmer community are now the legitimate owners of their land. There is some resistance from the landlords and mullahs who believe that we are not aware of what they challenge. They think that we are too weak in the rural areas and we cannot put our reforms into practice. To those who stand against our reforms, understand our warning that no one can stop the flood of the revolution. This flood would reach your homes and uproot all you possess. You will be destroyed and will never again be able to return to power. We will protect the poor farmers. We are here to stay, and as long as we are, we will protect poor people and defend their rights. It is their right to own the land which they plough with their sweat and blood. No one can deny their basic right. Long live the Democratic People Party of Afghanistan, the defender of the poor people's rights.

After reading the article Doctor Nasrat phoned Hamid to thank him for his article, but Hamid did not answer. He was in a deep sleep as he had spent most of the night giving finishing touches to the newspaper.

CHAPTER 40

Hamid sat in his office writing. This time it was not the usual communist literature, but about love.

Let love sharpen its teeth on my skin
Let love remind me that the world exists
Under your fingertips
I was away
Away from myself
Now I am here not empty anymore
I am full of you
I am you.

Love had filled Hamid's heart. Love forgives and forgets. He forgot about Safa's past as if it had never happened. She was pure to him again. As pure as love itself.

What a life. Up, down, up, down. Everything had happened so quickly. Hamid had been comfortable with his new role as the editor of a biggest newspaper when he went to Panjshir, where he was shot and almost died. Then when he recovered he declared his love to Safa, thinking that it was possible to love her and be with her, but his love was rejected. Now Safa loved him and he her. Other things were not important. The world was a great game and no one could predict what would happen next.

Safa was convinced that real love did only not require formal traditions and physical purity. What was physical purity if there was no purity of the heart and soul? It was purity of the heart and soul that kept the body pure. Safa promised herself to be the best lover to a man who was committed to help his country and his people and was prepared to lose his life for it. At that moment her soul and body were occupied by one man: Hamid. She believed in the second chance that Hamid had provided her.

Hamid did not forget family traditions and formalities. He sent his parents to Safa's house for *khastgari*, asking Safa's hand for marriage, but Safa's parents said that they could yet not say yes or no to this relationship. They needed to talk to Safa first and see if she approved or not. Obviously they were not aware of what was going on between Safa and Hamid. On their second meeting, parents of both families were delighted at the prospect of this marriage. The parents knew that both Hamid and Safa were educated and that counted much more than having large amounts of money or a high position. In reality, Hamid had a high position but not a lot of money.

A date for the wedding night was set. Basically it would be just three weeks after Safa finished her last exam and became a medical graduate: a junior doctor. In that case she could celebrate both her wedding and her graduation. The wedding night was only two months away and during this period Hamid and Safa were engaged. They met as often as possible, but not too much so Safa could continue to concentrate on her exams. Safa's graduation mattered for both of them. When they met, they did not make love, but had fun kissing. They were happy in each other's company. There was no need to rush things, since they would be married soon any way.

Their wedding night was organized in a wedding hall, a popular place among the middle class people of Kabul. There was music, dance, a mullah to read the wedding ceremony, excellent food and drink but no alcohol. Guests were from both families; and also friends of Hamid and Safa, who were mostly party members. These friends loved to celebrate with bottles of vodka, but Hamid had warned them that both families were religious and that they must respect the tradition of no alcohol. The wedding night was actually held in the afternoon. For security reasons, the government had imposed a curfew and most weddings now took place in the afternoon. By 6 pm, all the guests and families of the bride and groom hurried home before curfew began. For Hamid and Safa it was the same. They got into the car and told the driver to take them back to Hamid's flat. They had longed for this moment to be alone together, but as they left the hall, Hamid noticed that his driver took a different direction. He asked the driver where he was taking them. He responded that Doctor Nasrat had invited Hamid and Safa to his house for a drink, to celebrate the happiness of his two dear friends. Obviously for Doctor Nasrat it was not impossible to have a night code to let the newlywed couple reach his home without being stopped by a night guard. Hamid could not refuse the invitation. Deep in his heart he was happy to celebrate his wedding in the presence of a real friend.

The newlyweds had a real surprise when they reached Nasrat's house. A second wedding party had been organized in his house. The place was packed with guests, all of them party members. There was plenty of food, various types of alcohol, music and dance.

"You thought that I would let your wedding night end quietly, Comrade?" the doctor shouted from the end of the room. "I want all my Comrades to participate in your happiness, Hamid jan and Safa jan."

The house was full of people, male and female: all belonging to the People's Party. There was loud music and everyone danced and drank alcohol. For the first time Safa also had a sip or two. Hamid drank happily with his best friend, Nasrat. By the end of the night, when they decided to leave, Hamid was completely drunk. When they reached their flat, they made love. Hamid floated between the earth and the sky due to the effect of alcohol. He slept only for a short while and woke up to make love again and again.

Two days later they were shocked to hear the news of an unexpected event.

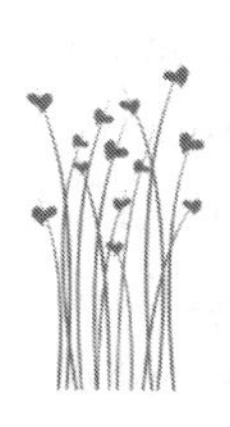 

CHAPTER 41

Rahmat had left for Pakistan. The night before his departure, he wrote two letters: one to his parents and another one to Hamid. In the letter to his parents he wrote how he could not accept the Russian invasion of his country. He did not believe that spreading un-Islamic philosophy and killing innocent people, who did not accept communism, was the right way. In the letter to Hamid he did not mention politics or the reason that he had left the country, but simply conveyed his brotherly love. When Hamid read the letter, tears came to his eyes. He knew the reason for Rahmat's departure; there was no need for his parents to explain.

Rahmat took the same route as Rabani, guided by one of Rabani's men, to reach the border town of Peshawar, Pakistan. For sometime Rahmat continued to receive code messages from Rabani, urging him to come to Peshawar and join the people in *jihad* against the infidels. No details of Peshawar or about a *jihad* were explicitly mentioned. The letters appeared to originate from the Balkh province in the north and mentioned that Azim, a friend of Rabani, invited him as his guest. The letters were written and signed by Rabani to show that they were genuine. Yet the province of Balkh and reference to different names of the writer were deliberately chosen to ensure that if the letter reached the hands of the secret police or the *Khad*, no one would find out that the writer was one of the most important leaders of *jihad*.

Rahmat noticed that the border town of Tera Mangal in Alaqa Ghair (no man's land) was a war zone camp. Men wore long beards, waistcoats with big pockets, carried AK47s on their shoulders and bullet belts around their waists. There were caravans of donkeys, mules, and horses, loaded with heavy weapons destined for Afghanistan. Rahmat couldn't believe his eyes. He had been informed that Afghan peasants fought the Russians empty handed or with weapons that they managed to capture from them. This border town presented a totally different picture.

Even wild western movies could not compare with this scene. The market was not only full of weaponry, but loaded with hashish, sold in large quantities from numerous shops. It was piled high in the front of the shops for everyone to see. Bigger stocks were available in the rear. Rahmat was tired and asked the guide whether they could sit in one of the cafes and have food and tea before proceeding to Peshawar. It was still a long way. They ordered and in the meantime Rahmat looked around for a basin to wash his hands. All restaurants in Afghanistan had a basin to wash their hands. It was part of the custom since in these parts of the world people ate with their fingers. However, here there was no basin. The guide noticed what he was looking for and told him that restaurants in border towns did not provide a washbasin. Rahmat stopped looking and joined the guide instead, sitting cross-legged on the hard wooden floor, covered by an old, grease stained *kilim*, torn in many parts.

As they ate he heard people speaking English with an American accent. He turned his head and saw three westerners, dressed in local clothes.

"Americans," the guide said with a smile, "they are on their way to Afghanistan."

"Are they not afraid of being captured by the Russians?" Rahmat asked, while he chewed on a hard piece of a kebab.

"Oh no, they won't go alone. They will be accompanied by our fighters. They are going to see for themselves how the war has progressed," the guide replied.

"I see, in that case it is not just our war, is it?" Rahmat smiled.

"No it is not. We have many friends. Arabs and Americans are our allies." The Americans sat down at a table not far from Rahmat. He watched them from the corner of his eye and noticed that they did not look like Americans or even foreigners. In fact, if they had not spoken English they could have easily passed for people of Noristan, with long beards and dirty, local clothes. Americans also did not need to wash their hands before the meal. They simply stuffed their mouths with pieces of meat, that wasn't so tender. Rahmat and his guide were busy talking when suddenly there was a sound of gunshots that made Rahmat duck for cover. This made the guide laugh out loud. He said, trying to sound serious: "Someone is just testing an AK47 before purchasing it. You will get used to this noise soon".

Rahmat was embarrassed and tried to hide his feelings. It seemed that it would take an eternity to get used to the smell, sounds and views of such places.

Close to where Rahmat and the guide sat, men smoked *chilam*, water pipe; there was a sound of boiling water each time they inhaled, accompanied with the strong sweet smell of hashish coming from their direction.

"It is amazing," Rahmat said smiling, "I can't see any police here."

"It is because of the British."

"What do you mean?"

"When India was conquered by the British, they left this part to its own devices. They could never rule this province anyway; so they left it as it was: as long as it was not a threat to the rest of India."

"So, how can anyone be safe here?"

"We are not, but the locals are safe. There is a tribal code of conduct. No one dares kill another because if someone is killed, revenge will go on from one generation to the next. A killing will be followed by revenge, and then a counter revenge of the revenge – and it will go on for centuries."

Different looking people arrived and left the restaurant. Rahmat was curious and watched as they told amazing stories in silence; he kept looking, totally mesmerised. A figure approached the entrance of the restaurant under a blanket. Since it was a hot day, surely the one under the blanket would be dying of thirst and heat. Soon Rahmat realised that the person under the blanket was a woman. He had never seen someone hidden like this before. In Kabul girls wore miniskirts. Although conservative women wore veiled burqas, they were not hidden and suffocated under a blanket, completely blinded and guided by a male.

The rest of the bus trip was tiring. In fact, the vehicle was a truck converted into a passenger bus with row of seats covered with hard plastic cushions. The road was rough and filled with many potholes, violently shaking its passengers. Some hit their head on the low roof from time to time. Rahmat developed a headache. When the bus finally stopped at dawn to allow the passengers to say their *namaz* at the roadside, he looked for some water. When he found water coming from an ablution tank, he did not even ask if it was safe to drink, he was so thirsty that he stood by it for a while quenching his thirst.

Finally, they reached the bus-stop of Peshawar city. From there the guide hired a three-wheeled rickshaw that could accommodate two passengers without luggage. The rickshaw stopped in front of a large, modern looking building. It was the headquarters of Leader Rabani, as he was referred to now. It was four stories high and painted white and pink. At the gate armed gatekeepers saluted the guide, obviously recognizing him.

They entered a wide corridor packed with people, some of them commanders of the Mujahidin in need of financial support, as well as arms, and others, simple refugees who were there to obtain tents for their families to sleep. They were waving their identity cards to identify themselves as refugees entitled them to monthly rations from the High Commission for Refugees. They reached the second floor and the guide led him to a reception room filled of men with long beards. Everyone sat cross-legged on the sofas, with their shoes lined up in front of them. Formal greetings were made between the guide and the receptionist, who immediately entered Rabani's office. When Rahmat stepped inside, Rabani rose from behind his desk and came to hug him.

They had a long talk. Rabani asked about Rahmat's family, how Kabul was these days and so on. Rahmat simply observed how strange it was to see Rabani occupying such a big office, a room filled with bulky furniture and with an aura of authority. The mullah of Andrabi had become the most important leader of the Mujahidin with connections to the Arabs and the CIA, receiving universal support. His headquarters was provided by the generosity of the Wahabis of Kuwait. Rabani informed Rahmat that he needed someone to take charge of the finance department and maintain an account of the money coming in and going out. This would not be an easy task. Money from the Arabic countries was not wired through bank accounts but in a more rudimentary fashion – in hand delivered briefcases, which Rabani himself carried to countries like Kuwait.

The briefcase always travelled empty and returned full, filled with nothing else but currency notes. The Arabs wanted the *Jihad* to continue and did not care about keeping track of the money. But for Rabani it was hard to see the money disappear so easily. He gave some to commanders to keep the war going, some for the staff at the headquarters, and, of course, some for this and that – always for hundreds of different reasons. He had established a finance department run by junior mullahs, but none were qualified in financial matters. Rahmat was a graduate of the faculty of economy and a man that he could trust.

Rahmat was provided with a two bedroom flat in a rather posh area of Peshawar called University Town, where the affluent lived, among them senior government officers, businessmen and rich smugglers. Smuggling was not only common in Peshawar. It was a respected profession, provided the smuggler was successful enough to own a house in University Town. The smugglers had the privilege of being neighbours to senior custom officers, who built their houses from corrupt money taken from smugglers through bribes.

The flat was air-conditioned. The smooth noise generated by the air-conditioner could easily lull Rahmat to sleep, had it not been the strangeness of being in a foreign country, away from his family and friends, thoughts that kept him awake for some time into the night. Instead he listened to the noise of the watchman banging his cane on the paved road; walking up and down and shouting *hoshiar*, be aware. This custom went way back to the times of Jahangir, the Mughal emperor, who had created the watchmen concept of patrolling the streets all night, to ensure the safety of its citizens, shouting *hoshiar*. Rahmat was not worried about his safety. He only missed his family. When sleep finally came, he dreamt that he was in Hamid's flat playing with his children: two boys, one that looked like him and the other that looked like Hamid. His mother also appeared in his dream, sitting on a couch watching them play as her eyes reflected her worries.

CHAPTER 42

It didn't take much time for Rahmat to understand that the previous system was not very professional. At the beginning he was nervous of being in charge of the finances, without any prior experience, but compared to mullahs, who though excellent in leading worshipers in *namaz,* had no clue whatsoever in financial matters. Rahmat could see that there were many lose ends. Not only were the accounts in bad shape, but the employees did not have the right skills, being either mullahs or fighters. There were qualified Afghan refugees on the streets of Peshawar looking for jobs, frequenting the office headquarters, begging the mullahs for a modest job to support their families with a basic salary. But the senior mullahs refused, because the jobs were kept for the members of the Muslim Brotherhood Party. The mullahs, previously simple keepers of their community mosques, had become very powerful after the Russian invasion, and now they, not the educated people, had the upper hand. Jealousy and inferiority complex drove the mullahs to stand up against modern education. They had spread the word that it was the educated people of Afghanistan who had encouraged the Russian invasion.

One day, when the office was crowded with long-bearded mullahs, wearing turbans, reeking of repugnant body odour of stale sweat, Rahmat overheard one of the mullahs:

"Yes brother, the educated son of donkeys sold our country to Russians."

Rahmat could not tolerate this comment. He raised his head, looked at the person who made the comment and snapped, "Mullah Sahib, where in the Koran does it state that education is wrong?"

Rahmat's expression was filled with anger. The mullah was caught off guard. He did not realise that the office housed a modern educated graduate from a renowned university.

"No, no. I meant only some educated people," The mullah said apologetically and continued, "You see Sir, the members of the People's Party inviting the Russians were educated people. I mean they are the ones to be blamed directly."

"But your comment did not refer to only one group of people. In your statement you mentioned all the educated people," Rahmat responded. "Whoever will not endure the affliction of learning, will forever stay in the debasement of ignorance," Rahmat quoted Ali, a cousin of Prophet Mohammad.

"I am really sorry," the mullah repeated.

Rahmat could see that the mullah was not really sorry. In fact, if he had not been in charge of the finance office and the only person responsible for the monthly salaries to the mullahs, if he had the same encounter on the street, the mullah would not have apologised. He would have probably confirmed rudely: yes, educated son of donkeys like you have brought the Russians to our country. Some months later Rahmat came to the conclusion that Kabul was in the hands of the communists and, Peshawar in the hand of the mullahs. Educated Afghan men who did not serve the communist government and who were also not members of the Muslim Brotherhood Party were demoralised. Not having a job, low self-esteem and poverty combined had forced them to take up arms. Leaving their families vulnerable in refugee camp tents; and by taking such patriotic actions they hoped that the Muslim Brotherhood Party would look after their family rations in their absence.

In August, Peshawar became a hot oven, baking the people. No one dared to be on the streets after 10 a.m. or before 4 p.m. People stayed in their offices and only moved around in their air-conditioned cars. Only beggars and poor Afghan refugees remained on the streets. As usual, Rahmat's office was filled with mullahs sitting on the couches with their smelly shoes lying in front of them. Then a boy with dirty, torn clothes entered the office and walked straight towards Rahmat's desk. The boy's face seemed familiar and when he looked at him more carefully he recognised who he was.

"Salam, Rahmat jan," the boy said.

"Salam, Asif. What are you doing here?"

"I came to see you. We heard that you were here."

"Where is Sharif?"

"Sharif went for *jihad* last year and never returned. He was killed near Kabul, fighting the Russians."

"Oh, I am so sorry, Asif. Sharif was a good friend. He was like a brother to me."

"We now live in Kachagari refugee camp. My mother asked that you come to visit us."

Rahmat immediately left the office and drove towards the refugee camp with Asif next to him. On the way he encouraged Asif to open up and found out how hard their life had been since they left Kabul and immigrated to Peshawar. Sharif had had no choice with the police in pursuit. Somehow the police had found out that he disliked the communists. If he went to prison, he would certainly lose his life. Ironically he didn't keep safe for long and was killed fighting for the Mujahidin instead. Rahmat remembered the day when Sharif had informed him of his departure from Kabul to Pakistan. He could not leave without bidding farewell to his best friend, even though his mother had strictly requested that their departure be kept a secret. Sharif trusted Rahmat with his life, a life in which his youth was taken away while he was far away from family and friends.

The camp was located far from the city. Rahmat had heard about such camps which had sprouted all around Peshawar, especially in remote areas. This camp was not considered to be a far commute and yet it took more than two hours for them to reach their destination. Rahmat could not believe his eyes. The camp was littered with tents: one tent was allocated per family, no more than five metres apart. There was no privacy. Each tent bore the logo of UNHCR. Some of the children played in front of the tents, their faces were covered in mud, their hair plastered with dust; dry lips, and stomach pulled in, rib cages visible – walking skeletons with shinny eyes. They probably fell into, what must have been open drainages running alongside the tents, while playing and chasing each other, without objections from an adults.

The only solid building in the camp compound was the mosque, built by the donations from Arab countries. The mosque was full even though it was not yet time for *namaz*. People also took refuge there against the hot backing sun. A flock of people gathered around a lorry where flour was being distributed. They pushed and pulled to reach the back of the lorry to grab a bag of flour. Some women and children fell while the other refugees stepped over them. There was no mercy and no kindness. Poverty and hunger had robbed them from such caring. Pakistani police used tree branches to hit the refugees into order, commanding them to queue in line at the back of the lorry.

Everyone was dressed in old, dirty clothes and Rahmat felt embarrassed to be the only person wearing clean attire. A shadow of sorrow flickered across his face. There was no sign of a school or a medical clinic. No education and no health care. They finally reached the tent that belonged to Asif's family. As they entered a heat wave hit Rahmat. The sun shone directly on the tent, making it hotter than a hamam. There was hardly enough space for the family. The two twins, one boy and one girl, both a year younger than Asif sat crossed-legged on a thin mattress. The floor was covered with an old kilim that was relatively clean. The entrance was filled with pots and pans, kept under a cloth against the flies. There were still plenty of flies buzzing around. The twins stood up and greeted Rahmat, bidding salaam. Gradually Rahmat's eyes got accustomed to the darkness that had swallowed the tent and noticed that someone was lying on a *charpaee*, bed made with wooden frame and rope.

Asif went towards the *charpaee* and called out: "Mother get up, Rahmat jan is here!"

A skinny woman with eyes deep in their sockets, yellow skin and face full of wrinkles, pulled herself up with difficulty and said, "Salaam Rahmat jan my son; so glad that you have come." Rahmat reached for her hands and pulled them towards himself, kissing them as a mark of respect.

"Your friend has gone, gone forever," the woman said, weeping.

"I am sorry. He was my brother just as you are like a mother to me."

"He missed you terribly ever since we came to Peshawar. Once he even said that he might try to go to Kabul secretly to see you, but he knew in his heart that it was only wishful thinking."

"Why did he join the fighting?"

"What else could my son do? There was no choice. We were desperate to get support from the Islamic parties, and the only way was by agreeing to send Sharif to fight alongside the Mujahidin. I initially opposed this, but Sharif couldn't accept the humiliation and poverty. One day he simply disappeared, leaving us some money. He promised to return but never did. Oh, my beautiful son, Sharif. How can I live without you?" she wailed.

The crying woman also made the twins cry.

"The hardest thing is that we only heard about his death months later. I didn't even see his body. I don't know where he is buried, or if he is even buried at all. Oh God almighty, have mercy on us." The women could not continue as she started coughing.

Rahmat couldn't fight back the tears running down his cheeks. He never imagined seeing the family of his dear friend in such appalling conditions. Sharif had lost his father many years ago and was the breadwinner of the family. He had then worked in a small workshop in Kabul, to earn whatever he could to support his family. Here in Pakistan he obviously had no choice. There was no work to be found and that was the reason that he had sacrificed his life, attempting to feed the family.

Rahmat sat down on the thin mattress on the floor. When he was offered tea, he refused. Sharif's mother was clearly sick. She was burning with high temperature. Rahmat insisted that she accompany him to see a doctor but she refused, obviously having lost the desire to live any longer. However, Rahmat continued to persist until the woman finally agreed. The doctor suspecting typhoid, ordered blood tests to be done. Rahmat dedicated his time that afternoon taking Asif with his mother to the doctor and laboratory, paying the bills and finally dropping them back to their camp. When he reached his home that night, emotionally exhausted, he could not sleep. He had completely forgotten about dinner. Lying in his bed his thoughts were about Sharif, the friend with whom he had grown up. Then his mind drifted to Hamid, his brother. He wished they could be together and protect each other. He missed Hamid very much. Hamid's face appeared periodically throughout the night and he kept praying: Dear God, please keep my brother safe. Please, dear God, please. Please, keep him safe in this vast terrain of stolen lives.

CHAPTER 43

Three days later, at around 4 pm, Rahmat left his office to go to Khyber Hospital to procure Sharif's mother's medical results. It was still hot and most of the people on the streets were Afghan refugees, trying to sell small things to make a living. There were men desperate to find a job, any job; hundreds of beggars competing with each other, running towards the cars, asking for money when they stopped, or going begging from shop to shop. Refugee children with dirty faces, dirty torn clothes, dusty long hair, were everywhere, begging for money and food. No one paid attention to these people.

Rahmat knew that desperate Afghan refugees were also involved in illegal businesses such as smuggling. They were used by the Pakistani mafia to smuggle anything including illegal goods and drugs. These refugees created an excellent business for the mafia bosses, who benefited from a win-win situation: If the goods were delivered, they creamed off almost all the profit and if the Afghan refugees were captured by the police, no one cared. The mafia was powerful enough to evade the law but the Pakistani jails were full of the Afghan refugees who worked for them. Horrific stories circulated about how Afghan prisoners were tortured by prison officers to make them give money to their keepers, who believed that these petty criminals were loaded. When prisoners became seriously ill, they died because they were not taken to hospital. Many Afghan women became prostitutes when they lost their husbands or male relatives in the war against the Soviet Union or natural causes such as illness. They slept with those Pakistani officials who were in charge of giving ration cards to the refugees. It was an incredible, pernicious system because although the rations were provided by the United Nations, their delivery system was controlled by Pakistanis. Even the United Nations knew that half of that food was snatched by Pakistani officials, but the UN turned a blind eye because they knew the officials could block the whole ration-giving system.

"Sir, please talk to the United Nations and ask them to channel support for the Afghan refugees through our party and not through the Pakistani government," Rahmat told Rabani one late evening when there was no one in the office.

"Why?" Rabani seemed to be annoyed by this suggestion.

"You know that half of the support for the refugees ends up in the hands of Pakistani officials."

"It is a minor problem."

"Sir, how can it be a minor problem when refugees are dying of hunger?" Rahmat used the term 'sir' to address Rabani these days because no one dared to call him mullah any more. Most of the people called him their leader.

"Look Rahmat, don't get involved with these issues if you want us to continue our jihad against the infidels who have invaded our country."

"I don't understand."

"I'll give you the whole picture. Stealing ration food from the refugees is nothing in comparison to what the Pakistanis get out of this war. All the money and support which comes from various countries for our jihad and for refugees are divided, and half of that ends up with the Pakistanis. You are an intelligent person and I am sure that you read in the newspapers that F16 fighter jets will be delivered from the USA to the Pakistani army soon. Do you know the reason for that?"

"Yes I can guess."

"You guessed right. The Americans bribe the Pakistanis by giving them everything that they want, to make sure the war against the Soviet Union continues. And if we want to stay safe in this country, we better not annoy the Pakistanis."

He entered the hospital with his mind flitting between thoughts of Afghanistan, Pakistan, his family, Hamid, the communists in Kabul and the Mujahidin in Peshawar; so he was not focusing on looking at the people in the corridor. Someone passed him and then shouted from behind, "Rahmat!" He looked back and saw his distant relative, Mohsen, who was some years older than him.

"Mohsen what are you doing here?" Rahmat shouted and opened his arms to embrace him.

"I just came here to get my lab results," Mohsen said.

"Me too, but not mine. What is wrong? Your health is okay?"

"Yeah, don't worry. This is normal for travel to the USA"

"USA?"

"Yes my sister sponsored me to join her there. You know that she has been in America for a long time now."

"Yes I know. Lucky you!"

"Oh, I am very lucky, especially since I came close to death."

"What?" Ramat asked with surprise.

"I tell you, it is not safe at all here and you better be careful."

"What happened, Mohsen?"

"We came to Pakistan about three months ago when the communists were threatening to put my father in prison for not cooperating with them. One day, I was walking on the street, going back home from shopping, when a jeep pulled up in front of me. Armed men jumped out of it, grabbed me by the arms and pulled me towards the car. I started screaming; asking people for help, trying to free myself, but no one came because they were afraid. One of them put his gun to my temple and said that if I continued shouting, he would shoot me. So I gave up and sat in the jeep."

"Oh almighty Allah, this is terrible," Rahmat said, shocked. "Who were they? What did they want? "

"That was the hard part. I didn't know if they were kidnappers or some other thugs until they took me to their prison."

"Prison?"

"Yes their prison. They were Mujahidin. I am sure you heard about their prison in Peshawar."

"So what happened after that?"

"They thought that I was a communist and spying for the Afghan government."

"No! Unbelievable."

"Yes, unbelievable. But I think the main reason that they thought I was a communist was that I had some personal friends in Kabul who were communists. You know that I follow Islam and go to the mosque frequently just like you."

"Yes I know. So what happened after that?"

"The Mujahidin have a prison here which is only for those people who are suspected of working for the government, including the communist. They, in fact, have jailed many people whose only crime is being educated. They think all educated people are communists. So you better watch out."

"Tell me how you got out?"

"It was just sheer luck. Someone on the street had seen me when the Mujahidin abducted me. He went and informed my father. It took him more than a week to find me. By then I had been tortured and beaten up every day, to force me to confess. But what I could confess? I was neither a communist nor a spy. Fortunately, my father has good connections among the Mujahidin. He even knows Rabani and with his help I managed to leave."

"What a horrible thing!"

"Yes this might happen to anyone; so please be careful. These days I never go anywhere alone. Someone is waiting for me at the entrance of the hospital. I must go now."

"Khoda hafiz."

"Khoda hafiz."

They hugged each other again and then Mohsen disappeared, leaving Rahmat feeling ashamed that he could not tell his relative that he was working for the Mujahidin, the same people who had put him in prison and tortured him.

As if all the troubles of the day were not enough, Rahmat was shocked by another revelation: Sharif's mother had tuberculoses. He was devastated. Who was going to pay for her treatment? Who was going to look after her children? What would happen if she were not treated and died? What kind of future would her young children have? The family was really unlucky. Sharif lost his father when he was a child and then he was killed in the war and now his mother was suffering from a very serious illness.

The incidents of the day, all sad and depressing brought him down and once again he could not sleep that night.

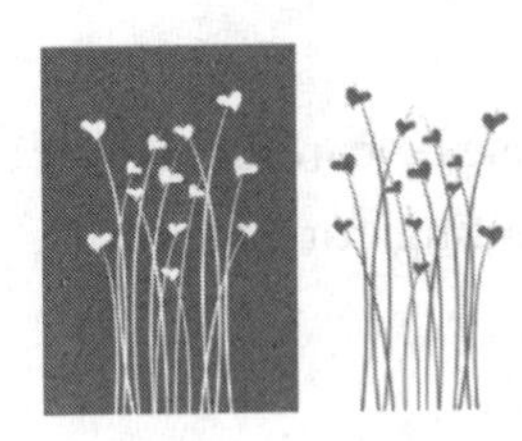

CHAPTER 44

Rahmat had come to the town centre one afternoon, to a place called Qisa Khani Bazaar, the bazaar of storytellers. But was it really a bazaar of storytellers, Rahmat wondered. He knew the history of Peshawar, once a crossroad and transit destination of various civilisations. Travellers and caravans stopped here on their way to China and India. It had been the centre of Gandahara Buddhism too, and not long ago, the winter capital of Afghan Kings. Now belonging to Pakistan the bazaar told a different story. Although it was no more than a kilometre in length, driving through it was a challenge. Waves of people passed through its streets. Taxis, rickshaws, horses, donkeys, bicycles, buses, and lorries were all its inherent features. Smoke came out from the many exhausts mingled with restaurant odours, making it rather difficult to breathe.

Crowded stalls on either side reduced the width of the road. Their owners sold anything from traditional clothes like the *shalwar kamis* to homemade desserts and *halva*. His eyes captured a banner of a semi-naked body of a European woman displayed on the walls of a local cinema. He had heard that such posters attracted many young men to the cinema. A boy, with a tray of cigarettes balanced on his head, suddenly rushed to the middle of the road in an endeavour to cross it without care, forcing Rahmat to brake hard to stop the car. The car came to a halt no more than a foot from injuring the boy. At last he reached Salatin restaurant and with difficulty found a space to park.

Male waiters with greasy, dirty clothes rushed about to serve the customers, normally referred to as guests. It was a two-storied building with smoke and noise originating from within. A waiter shouted when passing by that he should go upstairs, while rushing to deliver the order to another guest. Rahmat followed the narrow staircase and found himself in a room occupied by foreigners and women. Perhaps it was his appearance in clean clothes that led the waiter to believe that he deserved the best room of the restaurant. The restaurant was owned by an Afghan commander who led a Mujahidin group in war against the communist regime and the Russians. However, this Afghan commander activity was a smoke screen, as his real business was smuggling. Rahmat had previously met him at his salt market office location in Peshawar.

He went at Rabani's request to discuss financial matters. The storage of smuggled goods and the commander's office were in the same location. Rahmat noticed the rooms stocked with lapis lazuli and other gems, probably already on the smuggling route to Hong Kong and Bangkok. No attempt whatsoever was made to hide the merchandise. Even the police knew about it. The commander used at least some of his income for funding the *jihad*. Pakistan obviously supported the *jihad*, and didn't bother that the commander was smuggling heroin hidden among his lapis lazuli packing. The Pakistani government and Rabani simply shut their eyes. No one bothered to find out how the money came, what mattered the most was that at least some of it was used for *jihad*. The commander was, after all, looking after his own interest.

The top floor of the restaurant was divided into rooms without doors. Therefore, Rahmat could see three Afghans sitting next to two Americans, eating and discussing the war. From their conversation he gathered that the Americans were destined to travel to Afghanistan. Perhaps they were journalists or maybe that was just how they presented themselves. Many Americans ventured into Afghanistan in those days: journalists, mercenaries, CIA agents and even treasure hunters. The Afghan Mujahidin were looting museums and Americans were buying the stolen artefacts from them to sell in New York.

Whenever Rahmat missed home or felt depressed, he visited this restaurant. The food was delicious, especially the kebabs. Today he was feeling exceptionally depressed. A letter arrived two weeks ago. He ordered his meal and searched his pockets for the letter that he had already read many a times.

To my dear brother Rahmat jan, who is dearer than life to me,
I hope you receive this letter in good health and I pray that you are safe and happy. Your departure caused a great deal of distress to our parents and not a day passes without mother remembering you. I too miss you tremendously and feel the emptiness after your departure. I cannot provide further details about our life, but please do return for the sake of our mother.
Your brother,
Hamid

The letter was deliberately kept short since details could endanger both of them. If it fell in the hands of the secret police in Afghanistan, Hamid would be in danger and if it was read by the Mujahidin, Rahmat would be labelled as a traitor.

Rahmat had no desire to return home. Going back would be like a betrayal against his own beliefs. How could he return while the communists and the Russians ruled the country? And even if he agreed to go back to Kabul, he wouldn't be safe there. He was not convinced that his brother's contacts with the communist regime would be enough to keep him safe. Rather fate would likely lead him to being imprisoned or even killed by the secret police. Going back would also impose that he work for the communist regime. That was only on the remote assumption that the communist regime was tolerant enough to forgive him for the crime he committed. He would definitely be asked to join and work for the regime to prove his loyalty and that prospect was unimaginable for Rahmat.

The waiter arrived with his lunch. While he ate chopan kebab, mutton barbeque, his thoughts drifted from one place to another. He finished his meal but had not really enjoyed it. He asked for green tea in order to kill some time because he was still too early for his appointment. When it was time to leave he paid his bill and drove to the Intercontinental Hotel. Rabani had asked him that morning to apologise to a Sheikh, visiting from Kuwait, for his absence as he was going to the United States to meet important American politicians. From time to time, Rabani delegated such tasks to Rahmat, who was better equipped to receive foreign dignitaries, than the mullahs, who were clueless on interpersonal or international ethics. Dignitaries occasionally made donations to the Muslim Brotherhood Party and Rahmat was trusted by Rabani to receive the donations on his behalf. The truth was that, with an abundance of such meetings, Rabani could not attend all of them, and entrusted some of them to Rahmat.

The Intercontinental was the best hotel in Peshawar. As he appeared at the front desk, the receptionist recognised him as a frequent visitor. When he asked for the Sheikh, the receptionist guided him to a luxury suite. Sheikhs always stayed in big suites, because they never came alone. A butler or servant commonly used the extra room. The Sheikhs never liked their servants to be far away. What would happen if the Sheikh needed something in the middle of the night? Rahmat recalled an occasion when a Sheikh had rented a suite for himself and eleven extra rooms for his staff on each visit to Peshawar. He had even brought along his own doctor and driver. The butler let Rahmat into the suite and asked him to sit on the couch as he disappeared to an adjacent room. Perhaps he was helping the Sheikh dress, Rahmat thought. In the end he was made to wait for a long time. It came to a point that he was so bored that he became agitated and constantly and unconsciously adjusted his hair. A thought crossed his mind: should he write a letter to his brother? He had almost completed a full page, when he tore the page off from his notepad, crumpled the paper, threw it in a dustbin and in there he noticed an empty vodka bottle. It looked similar to the one in Hamid's flat. Assuming that the Sheikh would be embarrassed by the inspection of this scene he returned to his sofa.

Finally, the Sheikh entered the room. He was a tall man with broad shoulders, wearing a black robe over a long white dress and on his head, a typical white cloth tied with by a black silk ring, called keffiyeh. He looked impressive. His entrance was accompanied by a scent that followed the Sheikh, like an aura so to speak. Rahmat rose to greet his guest, but the Sheikh sat down, ignoring formalities. Rahmat felt nervous in front of this powerful man, presuming that many Sheikh dignitaries looked down at people like him, categorising them in the servant class. "So why did Mr. Rabani not come?" the Sheikh enquired, looking into Rahmat's eyes. Rahmat was prepared for this. While pressing the palm of his left hand with the thump of the right hand, clearly showing his nervousness, he replied:

"Your Excellency, he had to travel to the USA on very short notice."

"Well, I am disappointed. I wanted to talk about my further support of the *jihad*."

"Your Excellency, I will convey your messages to Mr. Rabani."

"No we must leave the issue of *jihad* for now. I was thinking of another issue that is related to refugees. We must support them too."

"Oh yes, your Excellency. You appreciate the casualties of Afghanistan against the communist regime, leaving behind widows and orphaned families in refugee camps."

"Exactly. Therefore we must act. I have thought of a good project."

"Yes, Sir."

"You must build a mosque in one of the refugee camps. Everybody must know that it will be a Wahabi mosque. Half of the money that I provide is to be used for the construction and the other half for the worshipers. Each person who enters the mosque must be provided with ten rupees, before each *namaz*. What do you think?"

"Oh yes, it is a great idea your Excellency."

After the conversation the Sheikh disappeared to the adjacent room and the butler returned with a brown package. He handed it to Rahmat, informing him that this was the money for the project the Sheikh had discussed. Rahmat put the package in his briefcase, thanked the butler and left.

He drove back to his office looking at the briefcase on the passenger seat from time to time. He imagined a mosque built of concrete, painted and decorated, furnished with bookshelves of the Wahabi movement. A mosque packed with refugees, among them would be Asif, a regular worshiper or a regular collector of ten rupees. His mind then switched to the bakery, where Asif would queue to buy two naans with his ten rupees, so that the family could have a dry bread dinner. Suddenly, he changed directions and drove away from the city. It was dark and unsafe to drive in Peshawar at night, but Rahmat did not appear to care. He was fed up with everything, including his life. Two hours later he reached the refugee camp, stopping in front of Asif's family tent. He went in, gave a bundle of money to Asif, informing him not to mention the source or the identity of who had given him the money. He returned to his car and drove home.

That night Rahmat dreamt of the day that his brother had avoided taking him to the snake charmer – yet their lives had always been the target of snake charmers. The world consisted of fools and snake charmers. Snake charmers had nothing to do with the snakes;

they hypnotised the fools who watched and were mesmerised with what they did. Rahmat wanted to run away, far away, where there were no snake charmers. But in his heart he knew that there was no escape from them, anywhere. As long as there were fools there would be snake charmers. They had the ability to attract fools, for as long as the world existed. The world stood on two feet: that of snake charmers and fools. Without one or the other, the world would be crippled. Without both, the world could be static. There was hierarchy among snake charmers within their respective communities.

The following morning Rahmat took a bus to the Afghan border. He carried with him only one small bag, some clothes and the Sheikh's money. He intended to ask his brother to use this money to help him and his family leave Afghanistan for a safer destination. He had thoughts of going to Europe.

EPILOGUE

Long after I had finished writing this book, I wanted to find out what had happened to the people I had talked about. I discovered that Hamid and Safa had escaped to Europe. But not with the money that Rahmat had stolen from the Sheikh. Rahmat was not with them because he had disappeared. Hamid and Safa were fortunate to leave the country alive. It was sheer luck. Before the communist regime collapsed, Hamid obtained a post as ambassador to Germany and he was there when the Mujahidin captured his country. Knowing that he could never return to Afghanistan because the Mujahidin would definitely persecute him, he applied for political asylum and received it. Now, like the changing tides, it was time for countries to change alliances. Suddenly the Mujahidin and their successors, the Taliban, were considered the bad guys. Hamid and his communist friends, who applied for asylum, became the good guys and in the way of the world, this too follows the story of human behaviour. Changeable.

I journeyed back to Afghanistan to try and trace Rahmat, but could discover nothing. He never made it home to Kabul to see his family and nobody knew whether he had been killed or not. Some said he was killed by the Mujahidin because he was running away with their money. Others rejected this version and believed that government agents, thinking he was carrying funds for the Mujahidin, shot him. While still others thought that he had been captured by bandits. The last rumour was that he had been killed by someone who was both a Mujahid, a government agent and a bandit. People changed sides quickly and were accustomed to wearing different coats. Afghans were a disturbed people. Can you blame them?

Of all the people, I especially liked Rahmat and I feel that I owe him something. It distresses me that I have been unable to conclude anything definitely about him. He vanished and till today, no one knows what happened.

ACKNOWLEDGEMENTS

Writing of this novel had many interruptions – my father passing away, my mother being diagnosed with cancer and my own health concerns. Nevertheless, life continued and I was blessed with love from those who not only believed in me but encouraged me in my journey and my love of writing.

I thank our young children, Sama – our beloved daughter, and Pedraam – our beloved son, who gave me the peace and space in our rather small cottage, to create the plot; my cherished friends, Alan Harmer and Kathleen Morf Vandervust, for their mentoring support and Susan Tiberghien, who founded the Geneva Writers Group and gently nudged me forward; my sister Nagina, who helped me to shape the novel, providing insights of the Afghan culture from the female perspective. I am grateful to my mother, who sowed my love of books early in childhood and to my beloved brothers Basir, Nasir (and his wife) and Nazir, for reading my draft manuscript and giving me valuable advice.

Thanks are due to my younger friend, Biljana Nicolic from Serbia, who translated the referenced poems of Mayakovsky into English. I cannot forget our family doctor, Isabelle Mottu, for regularly MOT(ing) my body engine to run smoothly through its health challenges.

I acknowledge my publishers Swarup Nanda and Chandralekha Maitra, and my editor, Oswald Pereira.

Above all, I could not have completed this work without the unwavering love I received from my wife, especially during this difficult period.

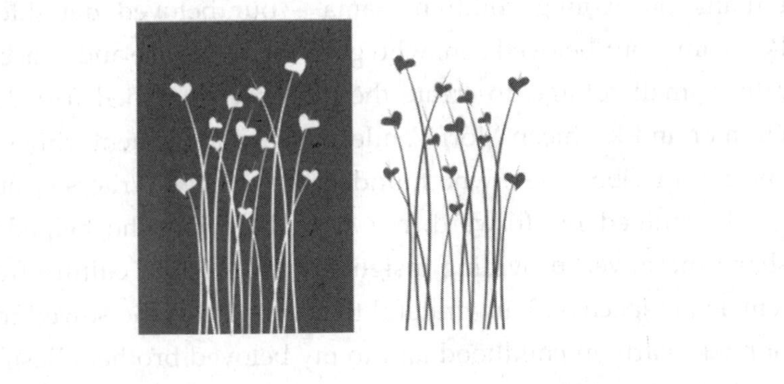

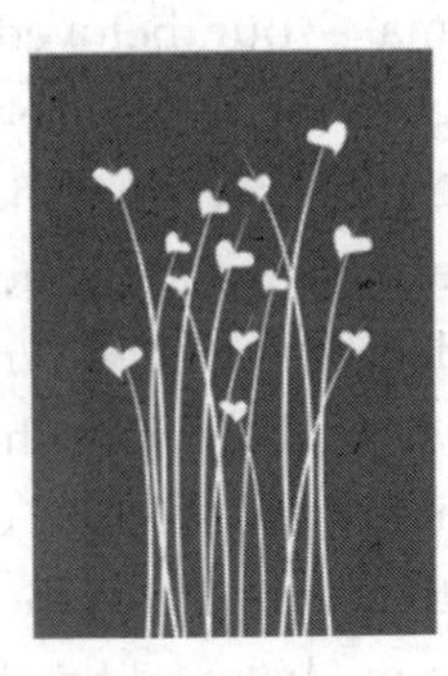